CHASTE BLOOD

BRITTNI CHENELLE

CONTENTS

1. Maddox   1
2. Sinna   9
3. Maddox   15
4. Sinna   24
5. Herod   30
6. Sinna   36
7. Maddox   44
8. Sinna   50
9. Maddox   56
10. Sinna   62
11. Delton   70
12. Sinna   77
13. Maddox   83
14. Sinna   89
15. Delton   95
16. Sinna   100
17. Sinna   109
18. Sinna   115
19. Maddox   122
20. Sinna   129
21. Maddox   137
22. Sinna   143
23. Maddox   150
24. Sinna   156
25. Sinna   163
26. Maddox   169
27. Sinna   174
28. Herod   185
29. Maddox   193
30. Sinna   200

31. Maddox   207
32. Sinna   215
33. Maddox   223
34. Sinna   230
35. Maddox   235
36. Sinna   241

Author's Note   245

ONE

———— M A D D O X ————

I jolted awake with the sharp, white pain of steel plunged into my chest. Nova's long, jet-black hair did little to hide the tears that fell down her cheeks. Her arms shook, driving the dagger deeper as sobs shook her body. The urge to cry out in pain, to wrestle the blade out of me and end the agonizing ache, was outweighed by my desire to watch her. The desire to understand.

"I'm sorry," she said, sobbing, but her grip never weakened.

Moonlight poured through my window, haloing her head and glinting off the top of the hilt as she held it firmly in place.

Why? Why are you doing this? I wanted to ask, but the blade had pierced my lung.

Am I dying?

1

My immortality fought to regrow the flesh around the wound, but the blade halted the regeneration. My thoughts moved to the night before, when Nova's body shook beneath my fingertips as she tightened to orgasm. I remembered how she sighed and kissed me, only to work herself up for another round. My thoughts raced through every second we'd spent together, desperate to find the moment that led her to this.

I had known she was special the first time we met. Herod had presented another batch of tributes and my eyes went straight to Nova. The same blue eyes that now willed my life to end, had lit when she first saw me, as if taken by surprise, just as they did now as she tightened her grip.

Nova lifted the dagger from my chest and plunged it in again, this time cutting into my heart. I coughed, wracked with pain as my immortality started to mend the first wound.

The adjustment was considerably more painful, but my lung was free. "Why?" I whispered.

She clamped her eyes shut, unrelenting.

My heart writhed, and each beat shredded the muscle against the blade. *You look so beautiful when you cry.* I wanted to reach out and wipe her tears, to tell her not to hurt, but I was frozen, confused, and in pain.

Then I understood this nightmare. *I am a fool.* I closed my eyes as laughter began to rise through the pain. I'd defended my actions to Ronan, assuring him that Nova was not my mate and that she meant nothing to me while, in reality, I was sure I was falling for her. Then, last night Nova whispered those three forbidden words, and they filled me with so much warmth that I was prepared to accept the consequences. Prepared to lose everything. My throne, my immortality, my life, just as my parents had, all for the one thing immortals couldn't have.

I suppressed my laughter, pressing my lips together to hold back my smile. The pain made me delirious, but my thoughts and memories were crystal clear.

I planned to stop accepting tributes from the other courts, a move that would publicly declare that I was in love, and therefore mortal. How long would we have before the Moon and Arrow Courts attacked? Or would it be the greedy gaze of my own people that led to my early end? I thought any measure of time where I could give myself fully to Nova would have sufficed and that the swell of release when I said those words aloud was worth letting the immortal world burn, but I could never have guessed that the girl who had stolen my heart might be the most eager to stop it from beating.

Everything we had was a lie, a ploy to make me fall in love so that my immortality would break and she could take my life. Laughter burst through my lips. The malice radiating through her blue eyes gave way to fear. I wasn't sure who sent her or if she'd made the plan on her own, but it didn't matter. She was the only one in the world I trusted, and she was a liar.

I wasn't sure what was funnier, that she never loved me or that I had thought I loved her. My immortality was strong and intact, a sure indication that I'd only felt a shadow of the real thing. As she watched me regain my strength, I realized how wrong I had been.

Her chest rose and fell so quickly that I could almost taste her fear. I grinned at her, pushing her deeper into despair.

She pulled the dagger from my chest. "Mad," she breathed, "I'm sorry."

I could see the war raging behind her eyes. I could see the dots connecting as she swallowed her failure, one breath at a time.

I leaned in and put my forehead to hers. "It seems that neither of us are capable of love."

"I-I do love you."

"We're beyond that game now, aren't we?"

Her sobs grew heavy. "Please," she begged, "Make me immortal, and I'll faithfully serve you forever. I promise, Mad."

"I don't believe you," I growled, my words dripping with malicious intent.

She grabbed my jaw, kissing me fiercely, and smearing tears onto my face. I allowed it, waiting for whatever I'd felt to come rushing to the surface, but whatever that feeling was, she'd struck it dead with that dagger.

Feeling my indifference, she pulled away. "Please, let me prove it. Tell me what I have to do. I'll do anything you want. I'll be anything you want me to be."

I lifted the dagger from my bed, handing it back to her. "I need you to be proof that the Blood King has no heart."

"Wh-what?"

"Stab yourself with this to prove your allegiance, and before you die, I'll make you immortal."

She swiped at her eyes with her free hand. "How can I trust you?"

"You can't, just as I can't trust you."

She tucked a strand of hair behind her ear, but her gaze was glued on the dagger as she considered her options.

"Are you going to save me?" she asked.

I brushed her cheek with my thumb and smiled softly. "We'll see."

"And if I don't do it?"

"We'll see."

She lifted the dagger, her shaking hands fragmenting moonlight off the blade and splashing it across the room. She lifted her chin, and her blue eyes bored into mine.

"Maddox," she whispered. "Don't forget about me."

I swallowed a lump in my throat, and with a sudden jerk of her hands, she plunged the dagger into her chest. Her eyes widened. She held my gaze until hers began to droop. I looked within myself for a memory, a feeling strong enough to push me to lean forward and bite her throat. A touch of venom was all it would take, but I felt nothing, not even as her life-blood spilled out of who I thought was my only ally, and on to my sheets.

"Please," she said, surprising me. "I love you."

A twinge of something stirred then. Like a wave,

it engulfed me, overrunning my thoughts and pushing my body into action. I lunged forward, sinking my fangs into her neck.

She wrapped a limp arm around me and whispered, "thank you," through gasps, but it was not love that I felt in that moment.

It was hatred.

Instead of pushing the venom through my fangs, I sucked, draining away her life before she knew she was going to die.

Her corpse lay still in my bed, and if I ignored the potent smell of blood on my sheets, she looked like she was just sleeping. Death was a mercy I regretted granting her, and I had to look away to stop myself from mutilating what was left. Ronan might grow suspicious. I wasn't fit to lead the Blood Court to absolute dominance. Not if I could be so easily fooled and manipulated.

I pulled off my torn shirt, tossing it into the fire. The less evidence Ronan could gather, the better. I called for a maid, and they promptly cleared the body away, changing my sheets as they routinely did with the tributes I'd grown tired of. I sat on my windowsill and stared mindlessly at the full moon.

I didn't care about Nova.

My wounds had already healed, but as the anger

began to wear off, sadness took its place. I was grateful for it. Only Nova could have taught to trust no one, ever. For the first time, I understood what Ronan had fought to teach me all my life. That love was nothing but a weakness designed to usurp immortal thrones. If I had been capable of feeling it, Nova would have succeeded in killing me. Whether she'd been my mate or not, I'd never know, and there was no use in dwelling on it. All that mattered was that I would never fall for it again.

Or so I thought.

TWO

I strained for breath, but the corset dug deeper into my sides. Of all nights, the royal dressers chose my divination ceremony to exact revenge. Years of snide remarks regarding their broken fashion sense went unaddressed, and tonight they were somewhere in the castle snickering about making my dress too small. I cursed under my breath, but whichever dark corner of the castle they'd slunk into was too far out of my range to retaliate with a spell. I tried one anyway. Several, in fact. It was birthright as a princess of the Shadow Court to wield magic and although I wasn't studious enough to conjure anything as flashy as a divination spell, nor skilled enough to fully shadow walk without a Hunter, I could certainly muster enough magic to ruin someone's day.

Ezra smiled to herself. "And who are we cursing today?"

But I was too invested in finishing my enchantment to respond.

She looked pleased and carried herself with a dignified grace I couldn't mimic. Her crown gleamed as she slid a pin through my hair to secure mine. Her golden skin and hair contrasted her charcoal lipstick and smokey eyes. She was radiant, but my sister hardly needed enhancements to look regal. She wore it that way because the color black was as bound to our history as the shadows that made up our home.

She reached for another pin. I wondered if she was going to start shoving random objects in there when she ran out. Still, I was happy to have some alone time with her before the ceremony. She had a calming presence that my sanity greatly relied on. The Queen of The Shadow Court didn't have to help me with my hair; we had people for that, but Ezra never missed an opportunity to be a good sister. I was lucky to have her. She was the only family I had left. She'd stepped into the role of Queen when our parents died, despite being only two years older. She was identical to our mother. I looked more like our mortal father, and I had the blemishes to prove it.

She was the superior beauty, as she had the superior heart.

I pulled down on my corset, hoping to move it enough to take a decent-sized breath, but Ezra's next pin dug straight through my elegant updo and into my skull. I swatted her hand away.

"I'm pretty sure it would stay on, even if someone punched me in the face."

She reared her arm back, balling her hand into a fist. "Should we test it?"

"I can't breathe. Can we have the dressmaker killed?"

She stepped back, giving me a once over. "I would, but you've never looked better," she teased. "Your face looks so pretty in that shade of purple."

She moved to my back and pulled at the strings until the corset popped open.

"Thank god," I said, gulping in air.

"If I loosen it, there will be a gap between the two sides. It might look... I don't know, sloppy?"

My ribs ached in response. "That's fine. I'll probably start a new trend."

She re-tied it looser than before and then grabbed another handful of pins. Instead of picking up where she left off, she stepped back, her honey-colored eyes narrowing as she scanned me. "I thought it was the dress, but you seem kind of nervous."

"No, of course not," I said too quickly. "What's there to be nervous about?"

She began circling me in search of a place to put her next pin. "Exactly. I changed the law specifically, so no choice needs to be made."

I wasn't about to let her feel sorry about this. She was too kind. I spun to her, grabbing her by her forearms since her hands were occupied with pins.

"You don't have to explain anything to me. I will always be on your side."

Her gaze dropped to the floor as she exhaled, but I could see some tension release from her shoulders. "I know. I just wanted to check with you since it's finally your turn. . . you know, in case that changed things."

I watched her, wondering how a person could be so delicate and so resolute at the same time.

"Tell me, if you still had the choice, what would it be?"

"Hunters. Easy choice."

"We'll see if you still feel that way after the tether takes hold."

"I know what I'm talk—" I stopped myself. "Tether?"

She stared at the granite ceilings, caught in her own memory. "When you see him..." She looked at me and raised an eyebrow. "Her?"

I shrugged noncommittally.

"When you see your mate for the first time, the connection comes to life. It's like an invisible string that ties you together."

I snorted. *As if this ceremony could get any more ridiculous.* But she'd piqued my interest, and I didn't want to miss whatever came next.

"You'll feel the pull of them until one of our Hunters takes them out. After that, it'll go back to normal."

I must've looked worried, because she smiled victoriously. "It usually only takes a day or two. You can handle it."

"Of course I can. You're working yourself up over nothing."

She smiled, dismissing her concern as she returned to her task. If the roles had been reversed and I had become Queen, I could not have handled it with half her grace. Yet, in typical Ezra fashion, she was worried about how her decisions affected me. When Ezra first changed the law to exclude the choice, I'd given her decision a lot of thought. My feelings were mixed at first. On the one hand, if our mother hadn't made the choice to seek out her fated mate, Ezra and I wouldn't even exist.

On the other hand, that choice was to blame for her death.

No, I was certain that even with a choice, I wouldn't be so reckless as to seek out my mate. Sending the Hunters to kill them was the best option, both for me and the rest of the Shadow Court.

I could tell that Ezra's decree weighed heavily on her, but I wasn't sure why. Our court would be extinct if not for that law. We'd seen the choice whittle our court away to almost nothing. Immortality was too important to toss away for a few short years of love.

So when the divination ceremony commences, and I steal a look at my mate, it will be my last. I will gladly send the Hunters to exterminate him and rule at my sister's side forever.

THREE

y throat tightened as the scent of mortal blood drifted into my quarters. Thirst choked me, and my mind fell into a haze. I might be a glutton for punishment, but I've always liked to delay feeding. I liked the unhinged feeling, the utter desperation, just before I gave in. That need was how I imagined mortals might feel in their final moments, desperate to cling on to one more shred of life before their bodies forced them into submission.

I could hear the scrape of Ronan's boots in the hallway growing louder as he moved toward my quarters to deliver the news, but there was no need. I could already smell what was standing in my throne room.

A knock sounded, and the door swung open. I stifled a laugh. His curly hair was ruffled, but his leather armor was neat and clean. I was amused by how little he did to hide his irritation. He had once been a well-respected Hunter for the Blood Court, but that was before the war ended, leaving a new set of royals to look after the Three Immortal Courts.

I didn't care much for Herod, the King of the Moon Court, or Delton, The King of the Arrow Court, but none of us wanted another outright war. We'd settled on the subtler battle of wills.

"Your Highness," Ronan said. "Herod has sent you some new tributes. They're waiting for you in the throne room."

My mouth watered as I stood, heading for the door.

"Should I have them drained for you?"

I stopped, giving him a sideways glance as I raised my brow. "No, I can manage."

"I just think you're playing a dangerous game. If one of them was to be your mate, you could risk—"

"I am not weak like my father."

My thoughts turned to the night Nova died, almost two years ago, as I stoked my fire with extra fuel.

"If I were to find my mate, I'd murder her without a second thought."

Silence was his disagreement. When Ronan

found out I'd killed Nova, he seemed relieved, but since then I'd indulged in a parade of tributes for extended stays at the castle to prove my indifference when I drained them. That had the opposite effect on Ronan.

His eyes narrowed, so I glared back at him. He might've been an old friend of my parents, but I didn't trust him or anyone else as far as I could throw them.

"Don't pretend like you're concerned for my immortality," I said, straightening my tie.

"I am. You have no heir. If your immortality is lost, the court will be lost as well."

Heir. I scoffed. Becoming mortal enough to produce an heir required finding my mate, but since he was vehemently against that, I was sure he was alluding to the second way. Naming one. I could choose a mortal successor and turn them into a vampire, but the number of times an heir dismembered and scattered the king to get the throne practically guaranteed that outcome. I could name someone who was already a vampire, but every one of them would see it overrun with new, greedy vampires who killed mortals for sport and would clear our town of the small pieces of civilization we were allowed.

I put my hand on his shoulder and he flinched. "I think you're bored. With all these tributes, there's plenty of blood to go around, and your position is practically obsolete."

His gaze dropped to the floor. "Before they died, your parents charged me with your protection."

I raised an eyebrow. "Then perhaps you should have given them this lecture."

I stalked out, refusing to let his irritation worm its way into me. I followed the sweet scent of mortal blood through the halls. I wasn't going to lose face with Herod just so Ronan could sleep better at night. The gifts that the other kings and I exchanged were supposed to be temptations, fulfill our lust, or in my case, thirst, but the chance of actually finding someone's mate was, well, zero. It was impossible. All immortals knew that, so our tradition was nothing but a harmless game, not to mention an endless supply of free meals for the Blood Court.

Two guards opened the doors to my throne room, and the warm, blood-scented air slammed into me. My tongue tingled as I focused on my throne, denying myself a view of the lovely tributes until I took a seat.

Herod stood at the foot of my throne, blocking my view with one of my guards at his side. Even using hushed tones, I heard my guard warning him not to shift. Not that there was any real danger for us if he did. The shifters generally couldn't defeat vampires in combat one-on-one. They moved in packs for that reason, but we outnumbered them five to one, and tonight, Herod seemed to be alone. The warning was unnecessary. He wouldn't dare shift in my territory anyway and risk losing twenty years of peace. I just enjoyed wasting his time. His gaze locked on me as my guard finished giving him the rundown. Herod's blue body paint looked purple in the dim reddish light of my throne room and I got a twinge of pride to see my court's customary color start to consume his. Not that I'd ever admit it, but I admired the shifter look--shirtless, free, and painted like warriors. I had once smeared blood down my lips and across my cheeks in a similar fashion, only to wash it off before anyone from the Blood Court saw.

I gestured to the guards. "Can we get Herod a shirt?"

He snorted, crossing his arms over his muscular chest. "A hundred years, and you're still not tired of that joke."

Of course, I knew that the members of the Moon Court dressed sparsely to accommodate shifting, but I'd never pass up an opportunity to give Herod a hard time, especially since this was technically an assassination attempt--a gift given with the intention of eventually finding my mate to make me vulnerable to death. The Moon and Arrow Courts sent me tributes more often than I sent them, but as the largest, strongest, and most influential court, they were right to target me. Ronan didn't understand that every tribute that was sent was confirmation of the Blood Court's dominance.

The tributes moved behind Herod, and I was tempted to sneak a peek at them, especially since the scent of the warm pulsing blood was so strong. The edges of my vision turned to a distinct crimson.

Herod cleared his throat. "Your Highness, please accept these lovely tributes as a token of the Moon Court's respect."

He moved aside and I nodded in appreciation before allowing myself to appraise the tributes.

Five women stood in the center of my throne room, donning white gowns that differed slightly, complementing their unique features. Like delicious morsels wrapped in shiny foil, each was lovelier than the last. They'd all end up the same way, a bloodless corpse, but from their confident and seductive smiles, it was obvious they each believed themselves to be the exception.

Herod smirked and nodded to one of the girls. She was an inch or two taller than the rest, with jet black hair, blue eyes, and a smoldering presence. I knew exactly why he thought I'd like her. She looked a lot like Nova. I wasn't surprised that word had gotten to other courts that I had kept Nova for so long, but I was surprised how frequently his tributes resembled her, even years later.

Each time I took to a tribute for an extended period, Ronan would be convinced that I'd found my mate and that we were all in grave danger. He'd check for signs of my immortality waning, but Herod had continued to bring me a specific type as if he knew she had been different from the others. His opinion hardly mattered.

I was more concerned with Ronan as his nagging affected my daily routine. I hoped as the years passed, Ronan would come to learn what I knew all along. Regardless of their beauty, it always ended the same way, with a bloodless corpse in my bed.

I took a long look at each tribute and saw the same hopeful expression plastered onto each of their faces. Their gazes all screamed the same two things.

Make me immortal. Make me a queen.

If they had any sense at all, they'd know that royalty would never beg to become so, not even with their eyes. If they really knew what I suffered, they wouldn't wish for it.

There were so many at my disposal. So many who would murder me if I let my guard down.

Everyone wanted a bite of my throne.

One of the girls shifted slightly, drawing my attention. Her hair was chin-length and light in color. Her bangs hid her eyes, and although I couldn't see her well, she set off an alarm in my body. I felt my fangs sharpen as heat tore through me and I sprung from my throne. I stalked over to the girl. She was a few inches shorter than the rest and far less curvy.

The girl wilted beneath my stare. I pushed her bangs out of her eyes to get a clear look at her face, and she winced. I was horrified by what I saw in her softly curved features.

Herod came up beside me. "Good choice, Sire, this is—"

I spun with bared teeth, the pulse of his neck pulling in my full attention. He growled, which intensified his appearance, as if his body was itching to shift.

"What's wrong?" Herod asked, crouching defensively.

My legs shook. "Return this tribute to wherever you found her."

Ronan stepped between us. "What is it, Sire?"

The words sickened me before I said them. My stomach churned with unease.

"The tribute..." I said through bared teeth. "She's not fully grown."

Herod's eyes widened "My apologies. She said she was—"

"Look at her!"

Herod's gaze dropped to the ground. I headed for the door, my appetite soured, as Herod called after me, his words lost in the torrent of my rage.

FOUR

— S I N N A —

I held my head high as I entered the dark hall and stepped out onto the black carpet that stretched out in front of me. Our court's Hunters stood at attention on either side; their solemn expressions breathing intensity into the sound of the drums as I approached. The Hunters were dressed in black armor that looked similar to their usual set; only tonight they had silver swirls embroidered into the collars and around the seams. I scanned them for one in particular but didn't see him.

The lethally trained men and women were muscular, and stood unnervingly still, which seemed to grate on my confidence, but once I recognized a few of them from various nights of indulgence, the intimidating formality of the ceremony lifted in my mind. I eyed each one as I passed, admiring their strength and versatility. If I had one regret in life, it was that I was born royal and, therefore, could not become a Hunter myself. They might've had to kill innocents, but their brave actions ensured our court's immortality, not to mention they were able to roam above ground with the mortals as long as they reported back on time. They had our lives in their hands and they seemed incapable of failure, never before missing a mark they'd been assigned to eliminate. The closest I could get to being a Hunter was the occasional night time interlude, a glimpse or two at their vicious training regime, or a nugget of information gleaned from Finn in exchange for sexual favors.

My attention snapped to Finn when he finally came into view. Despite keeping his eyes trained directly ahead, he bit back a smile. His shaggy hair was messy, his clothing wrinkled, and unlike the other Hunters and their neutral expression, he seemed more than a little inappropriately amused. I spent my nights with various Hunters for variety, but I called on Finn most due to both his adequacy in the bedroom as well as his aloofness and discretion outside of it. We'd made a deal that I'd select him for the honor of eliminating my mate, and in exchange, he'd regale me with the play-by-play of my mate's death, as well as a detailed description of the world above ground. I wasn't sure why, but I felt embarrassed by the possibility that my mate might beg for his life in the end. A mate was in some ways a reflection of oneself, and while the other Hunters would hide a detail like that from their report, Finn would tell it to me straight.

Ahead, I spotted the pool of foresight, a beacon of shimmering light in a comfortably dark world. As I neared, my thoughts moved to my sister's ceremony.

I remember the anxious energy that hung in the air as she took a silent moment to look into the face of the man reflected in those magical waters. I remembered how carefully the Alpha Mages watched her as she drank in the visage of the only person she could truly love. Knowing what my sister would choose, I promised myself I wouldn't look. After all, he was unwittingly in his last few days alive, but when the glowing ripples settled and my sister leaned forward, I caved and gaped at the man who looked back at her. He was pleasant looking, but ordinary as all mortals were. He didn't have the divine beauty of immortality like my sister, but his youthful energy shone through his warm brown eyes.

As expected, Ezra ordered a Hunter to eliminate the visage without hesitation, and we hadn't spoken about it since. I could barely recall the man's face in my mind's eye, but I could never forget the kindness in his smile. Every now and then, I saw it reflected in my sister.

I was fortunate not to have the choice. Fortunate I'd never have to wonder about the person I saw reflected in the magical waters. The drums echoed through the darkness, synching up with my heartbeat as I prepared to glimpse one of the few experiences I'd ever be denied. Like becoming a Hunter or visiting the world above, I'd learn to live without this. Without my mate.

Ezra cleared her throat. I jolted to attention, lost in my own thoughts. My sister stood at the far edge of the circular pool, and the glow of the water splashed onto her beautiful face. The Shadow Court's Alpha Mages all grasped the granite edge of the basin, their eyes transfixed on the water as they focused on their forthcoming task.

Ezra's eyebrows rose slightly and she shot me a wondering look. I forced a grin. When she reciprocated, I felt mine grow into a genuine smile. *This is just my first of many.* I knew a new mate would surface for me every hundred years or so, so this ceremony would become a tired routine eventually. I just had to get out the jitters of the first one.

I stepped up to the edge of the granite pool and could see that the water was only a foot or two deep. I squinted as they adjusted to the light, which flickered whenever one of the mages moved their hands through the liquid. I was proud of our court's unique ability to divine mates, though I was grateful not to have to endure this procedure daily for each member of the court. The Alpha Mages, or Diviners, as they were sometimes called, were well respected in our society, but the labor they did was intensive and endless.

Ezra raised her hands, and the drums silenced. "Today is a very special divination ceremony as it is the first for Princess Sinna. Our court was nearly eliminated by the temptation to abandon life for fleeting and meaningless moments of affection, but now that our court has chosen life over defeat, we need not burden ourselves. I ask that we all reflect on today as a celebration of life and prosperity for the Shadow Court and all who belong to it."

Applause filled the dark hall, and for the first time I could feel how vast our audience was. I took a steadying breath as I prepared to look into the face of my mortality.

"Have no fear,"Ezra said. "Our Hunters will not fail to protect you."

"I am not afraid."

Her expression softened as she watched me. "Then let the ceremony commence."

FIVE

*M*y nostrils flared as I stepped back into the moon's light, the wolf within tore through my human skin like a child unwrapping their first Christmas gift. The cobble-stones cooled my paws as I slunk through the shadows towards the wood. *How dare he?* I'd vetted each of the tributes. Knowing the Blood King's sensitivity to age, I'd triple-checked each one. The girl was admittedly a bit underdeveloped for her age, but for him to insinuate that I'd violated the terms of our treaty was a testament to his arrogance. I stepped through the tree-line, but my wolf was too enraged to allow me to move any farther away. I wanted nothing more than to topple his reign and rid the world of those blood-sucking monsters that considered themselves superior. I turned back and glared at the cathedral they called home. The metallic scent of blood was bearable in my human form, but as a wolf, it burned my nose, stretching further than a mile radius around their base. If I moved any closer I would struggle not to gag from the smell.

I watched as shadows passed in front of the stained-glass windows, digging my claws into the leafy terrain at the edge of the city. The futility of my desire to retaliate kept me from returning home. Even if the Blood King was dumb enough to step outside alone, I wouldn't be able to do more than injure him. Instead, I paced in the shadow of the tree-line, imagining what it would feel like to hear King Maddox cry. A branch snapped, and I bared my teeth at the sound.

Ronan stepped into view, cradling the unconscious tribute in his arms like she weighed nothing. My father's favorite pastime was recounting tales about the war that caused this pyramid system and won the Blood Court its position on top. Ronan was a key player in every story, a brawler through and through.

He didn't look like much to me, but the way he so

casually approached me while I was in wolf form spoke volumes of his lethality. The girl in his arms was so still that I thought she might be dead, but I could still hear the pulse of her beating heart. King Maddox trusts this guy to return her unharmed? I eyed her warily. Ronan moved closer, so I bared my teeth, but instead of fear, he spoke casually.

"The king is in a mood tonight. I'm ever so sorry for his outburst." The unmistakably metallic scent wafted from his breath.

I growled as I decided whether it would be worth the trouble to tear his limbs off.

"Perhaps it's time to give up your search. These tributes never yield results, and I'm sure it's been exhausting collecting them to no avail."

This time when he spoke, the moonlight shone off of his red teeth. My gaze moved back to my failed tribute, and I shuddered as I listened more carefully. Sure enough, the heartbeat I'd heard coming from the tribute had tripled in speed. It began to skip beats and her body jerked in Ronan's arms. He did not so much as look down at her. Instead, he stepped into the tree-line, as if the woods were safe and not a blatant disregard for my court's territory.

I felt a new consciousness slip into my head as

one of my fellow wolves neared us, then another, and another, but Ronan turned away and stared at the moon as if lost in thought. A collective growl echoed through the wood as a handful of wolves surrounded us. Ronan's dinner went still as her heart beat one final time. The lone vampire snapped from his daze. He looked up at my pack, his attention moving from the moon-white fur of one pack-mate to the other in detached appraisal.

Finally, he sighed deeply. "It seems my meal's gone stale."

Ronan tossed the corpse, and it landed with an empty thud at the feet of my pack. Tren leaned in and sniffed at it before his gaze moved to me.

His thoughts rang in my head. "What are you going to do?" he said through the link. "You going to let this bloodsucker disrespect us like this?"

"Fall back."

"You can't be serious."

Kay's voice cut through. "Tren, he's right. That's Ronan the Brutal."

She glared at Tren. She was my number two, and the only voice I didn't mind having in my head.

Ronan turned his back to us, and Tren lowered to the ground.

"Well," Ronan said, "I'll get going. I suppose I'll see

you at your next offering. Make sure you're conscious of their ages. She did taste a little young."

I gritted my teeth.

"Now, Herod! While his back is turned." Tren said, but his voice was less sure than a moment ago. "He can't take all five of us."

Kay's voice was harsh. "You can't smell how many of them are around? Your alpha said fall back, so fall the fuck back."

Tren's head lowered as we all watched Ronan walk down the hill to the chapel. It was a gut punch to us all.

As a new alpha, I didn't have the benefit of having ever fought a vampire, but I wasn't willing to risk the lives of our people by underestimating one. Especially not one known for his exceptional combat skills. The Blood Court had the unique ability to bite and turn mortals, increasing their numbers, but they did so with caution. One should always be cautious when giving the gift of immortality to any mortal being. Even so, that advantage had won them the war. The Moon Court's ability to shift, communicate with our pack telepathically, and hunt anything as long as we had a scent, wasn't enough to change the status quo.

Before he passed, my father had taught me how to choose my battles. It might've seemed too passive to Tren and some of the others, but there was only one way to eliminate the Blood Court, and that was finding King Maddox's mate.

SIX

*T*he Diviners lowered their hands to the bottom of the glowing water and began to hum. The even tone swelled through the hall as I locked my gaze on the center of the glowing pool. My heart beat so quickly that it pushed the air from my lungs, and I clenched my jaw to steady my body from shaking. No matter what I felt when the image appeared, attraction, lust, sadness, fear, humiliation. . . I'd only need to endure it for a moment. *I can endure anything that long.* Finn was waiting to erase my mate from existence, to spare me one hundred years of wondering or a few blissful years of knowing before an abrupt and eternal end.

The pool's light brightened as the Diviners poured their magic into it. During my sister's ceremony, I'd seen the way the white of the Diviners' eyes overtook their irises and pupils. I'd watched the granite basin glow like the moon, filling every crevice of the hall with cold, white light, but now that it was my turn, I could not enjoy the splendor of the event. Curiosity clawed at my mind, rendering me incapable of looking anywhere but the center of the pool for fear I'd blink and miss it.

A red hue brushed the surface of the pool, and I leaned in as the blurred image took form.

All went still.

Dark wavy hair covered his face, obscuring all but plump red lips. Every nerve in my body writhed against the sensation. The urge to turn away was maddening, like leaning too close to a campfire in order to fully savor the relief of cold air on your cheeks when you turned away, but I didn't dare to move. Paralyzed by the instantaneous tethering of my life to his, I longed for relief. I longed to feel the lines cut and the release of his hold on my existence. The pull was immediate and powerful. I hadn't even seen his face. My body pulsed. *Please. Look at me.* As if I'd said the words aloud and they'd somehow carried to him, he lifted his chin, his gaze lifting to meet mine.

I felt naked, swallowed by the charcoal black of his eyes. One glance and I knew something had gone terribly wrong. This was no blemished mortal threatening my existence but a divine entity. His dark eyes were rimmed with red, and his jawline was sharp and smooth as polished stone. The tether tightened, fortifying itself with his details as I drank him in. Emotions overran me, filling my body with their toxic mixture until I landed on the only one that mattered, a dark and intense hatred.

My jaw ached, but I didn't dare unclench it. As if he'd sensed the fire he'd lit inside me, his red lips stretched, turning up the corners of his wicked mouth. Joy filled his whole face, but even that couldn't light the pitch blackness of his eyes. Then his lips parted and the nightmare I didn't dare to imagine slipped into reality. Two gleaming white fangs revealed themselves, plunging the Shadow Court into utter chaos.

The light of the pool was snuffed out and the image along with it, but it was burned into my mind as the shrieks and screams of everyone in attendance reached me, jolting me from my silent stasis. The sound rattled my bones as the shadows closed in and my legs buckled. I felt strong hands close around my arms, as a thousand people rushed the pool.

"Finn!" I screamed, but my voice was engulfed by the others.

I screamed again, the only indication a fresh scrape of soreness against my throat.

Then I felt the soft brush of lips against my neck. A chill ran through my body. The lips moved against my neck again, and this time I was sure they belonged to Finn. Bodies barreled into us as Finn grabbed my hand and led me through the crowd towards the exit. I lifted my free hand with every intention of casting something, anything, but before I could, a light cut through the shadows and silence fell on the hall.

Ezra held her hand above her head, light beaming from her palm.

Her voice was amplified and strong. "We will consider our next move carefully. This situation will be dealt with appropriately. I assure you, the Shadow Court's survival is of the utmost importance."

But Finn didn't stop to listen. He pulled me out of the hall, through the tunnels, and didn't stop until we were alone, panting in my quarters with the doors locked behind us.

"The Blood King," I said, fighting to catch my breath.

"I know."

"It's the Blood King!" I turned away, trying to settle my thoughts.

An immortal mate? It wasn't possible, yet the pull of the tether on my chest was unmistakable. Why hadn't anyone prepared me for this possibility? Our Hunters were lethal, but they had no chance in hell of killing an immortal, let alone the leader of the most powerful immortal court in the world. Did that mean I had to suffer the tether forever? The Blood King. The fucking Blood King. He was a ruthless killer; everyone at the Blood Court was. I hated him. I hated every disgusting monster in his demonic court. What did it say about me if I was mated to one?

"Calm down."

"You promised you'd kill him. I'm going to be stuck like this. . . with this feeling."

Tears sprung to my eyes. Reeling, a new mouthful of despair filled me with each breath.

"Calm down." He inched toward me.

"Don't tell me to fucking calm down. Fix it, Finn! Make it not hurt."

Without hesitation, he unsheathed his knife. My bedroom's light caught the edge of the sharpened blade. I watched with detached curiosity as he closed the gap between us with his weapon drawn. He claimed my mouth, his tongue sliding between my lips. Stunned, I forgot about his knife until my body was jerked upwards along with the slice of his blade. I broke the kiss, and the small space allowed my dress to fall to the floor, its strings frayed where Finn had cut them.

I heard a zip, and he peeled off his armor and tossed it aside. A valiant effort, but my situation was hopeless. My heart seized as my thoughts returned to the ceremony, and I took a defeated step back.

"It's not going to work, Finn."

He shoved me back hard and I scrambled to keep my balance, only for my bed to hit the back of my knees, sending me toppling backwards. Finn stepped out of his pants, his body sculpted to perfection, his honey-colored eyes ablaze with desire. *Stay in the moment. Be present.* I closed my eyes and felt the flat of Finn's blade press against my stomach. My breath pushed my body against it, and I liked the coldness of the steel as much as the danger. It lifted, and my bra popped open, spilling tiny glass beads across my bed.

The lips that had found me in the chaos now trailed down to my lace panties, which he tugged with his teeth. I covered my face with my hands, so I could wipe away any tears that dared to slip out. Finn would fix this, just like he fixed everything else. I just had to trust him.

"Faster," I begged.

"Yes, Princess," he said, as he straightened and cut them off with two fluid moves of his blade.

His hands were hot as they tightened around my waist from where he stood at the foot of the bed. Before I had time to brace myself, he drove into me, pleasure bursting between my legs. My back arched to deepen the pleasure with each powerful thrust of his hips.

"Yes," I breathed. "Hurt me."

His fingertips pressed into my sides as he gritted his teeth and pushed deeper to obey. Pleasure crawled up from the bottom of my spine and escaped in a moan that made Finn's pace increase. He dropped his chin, his focus waning as his body's instincts took over.

"Don't you fucking dare!" I said through gasps.

He grunted a reply. I wasn't done yet, not by a long shot. Not until my body gave out. Finn's hair slipped forward, casting shadows across his eyes. My heartbeat stuttered. They looked charcoal black. A flicker of pleasure sent sparks onto the fuse.

Focus Sin, stay present. "Harder!" I cried, hoping Finn could pull me out of my head.

His muscles flexed, but I had already returned to the ceremony in my mind's eye. Charcoal eyes. A wave of pleasure slammed into me. Bloodstained lips. My body bucked, straining for release. A smile stretched across a statuesque face, revealing the sheen of pointed fangs. I closed my eyes, desperate to make the memory stop, but that only strengthened the image. Finn was gone, and in his place, the Blood King smiled wickedly down at me, pushing me to orgasm.

SEVEN

I doubled over the pristine porcelain as fresh, blood-stained bile shot from my mouth. I hated the red splatter almost as much as the sick feeling that claimed my focus.

I could hear Ronan's voice through the door. "The King is ill. Don't return until morning."

I wiped my mouth and stood upright to get a look at myself in the mirror. Blood dribbled from my chin, but otherwise I looked normal, and not nearly as sick as I felt. I splashed my face with water. *Fucking Herod*. The gag-inducing sensation rose up so quickly. I'd barely held it in until I made it to the bathroom, despite only being a few yards away.

He had fucking poisoned me. The last thing I needed was to appear weak, not while the literal wolves were circling, and whispers of my own people were second-guessing my every move. If Herod was bold enough to try a move like this, perhaps Ronan was right about how casual our relations with the other courts had become. I'd always considered the war to be foolish. It resulted in the dismemberment of all of the monarchs of the immortal courts and the total elimination of the Shadow Court. I thought the tribute system would allow us to compete with a battle of wills, without resorting to the violence that orphaned us all, but Herod had gone a step too far.

Even as the nausea subsided, the weight on my chest remained. What the hell had he slipped me? If I could find the smallest shred of evidence, I'd have grounds for war, and my court would only praise my ruthlessness.

I flushed the regurgitated blood and cracked open the door. "I want you to test the tributes for poison."

"Sire, they've all been tested. I sampled each one before delivering a single drop to your chamber."

"He poisoned it. I'm certain."

"Perhaps you just need some rest."

I grabbed a towel and wiped my face with it before I followed him into my chamber. I flashed my fangs. "I want them retested."

"Yes, Sire."

I took a seat on my bed. "And what of the young girl? Did you return her?"

"Yes. She was heartbroken that you didn't allow her to join the court and make her immortal."

"See to it that Herod stops promising them that. It only makes the tributes more irritating."

He bowed. "Will that be all?"

The pressure in my chest flared, so I waved him out. I took a steadying breath. It was odd how mortals craved eternal life, like immortality was the opposite of death. But a true immortal knew better. The opposite of death was life and immortals were barred from both. Ever since my parents died, I had resented their decision to surrender their immortality. I always assumed they knew something about what it meant to live that I couldn't understand. Only now, as I lay with my hand pressed to my chest, I could feel Death's presence. He was not nearby, but I felt his existence on the edges of my illness. I savored the feeling, like a fine wine washing over my tongue.

I closed my eyes until the sensation passed, but a fragment of the feeling lingered, like the memory of a dream. My thoughts moved to Nova, her blue eyes, and the tribute who vaguely resembled her.

Perhaps I was too eager to feed on tonight's tributes, too stubborn to admit to Herod that he was right about Nova. Regardless of their similarities, and how they dulled the ache of her absence, I didn't want him to fill my throne room with blue-eyed imitations of her. I'd barely even looked at the others, and in the silence, my thoughts drifted to places I tended to avoid. It would have been nice if, just for tonight, I had someone begging for immortality if, for no other reason, to remind myself it was mine to give.

The sun was setting when I woke, but I could still feel the frigid glare in the last of the sun's light, through my red, stained glass window. I liked to wake after it dipped below the horizon, but based on how low it hung on the horizon line, I'd only risen a few minutes early.

I made quick work of my nightly routine, and as expected, Ronan waited for me outside my door.

"How are you feeling, Sire?"

"Fine." We walked together through the hallway. The portraits of my ancestors glared at me as I passed.

"I've retested the tributes and couldn't find a trace of poison in any of them. Perhaps you overindulged?"

47

I glared at him but didn't slow my pace. "Or perhaps it was you who tried to poison me."

He sighed. "Seems rather pointless, wouldn't you say?"

"Send thirty of our soldiers to the Moon Court to tell Herod we won't be accepting tributes for the next month, pending an investigation of his recruitment methods."

"Thirty, sire? Surely the Moon King will consider it a threat to—"

"It is.

"Perhaps a more diplomatic—"

I flicked my hand, stopping him short without so much as looking in his direction.

He cleared his throat. "The Clan is assembled in the study."

I turned in a huff and headed back up the corridor. "Lead with that next time."

The study was by far the stuffiest room in the refurbished cathedral. The drapes were black, the furnishings jewel-tone velvet and the fireplace always filled with ashes, though it was never lit.

As ever, the Clan was seated on one side of a long table, with my vacant throne at the center. The set up resembled depictions of the Last Supper, but with a few important differences. Each of the vampires in the Clan was blessed with ageless beauty. They were less like companions and more like a company of betrayers, and instead of The Messiah, Satan himself sat on the throne. This was not a court of round tables and equality. The highest-ranking Clan members sat at the center, and the lowest sat further toward the edges.

It was the ideal arrangement for reviewing candidates for immortality.

I took a seat at my throne beside Aiko, who had been my right hand since I was crowned. She bowed her head in greeting. Peng sat to my left. He was next to inherit my throne if I didn't choose an heir, and therefore my biggest threat. He grinned at me, not for kindness' sake but to flash his fangs. I reciprocated, and a moment later, the double doors opened and a mortal was ushered in.

EIGHT

*E*ven as I buttoned my jeans and straightened myself up in my bedroom mirror, Finn lay sprawled naked across my bed. I thought he might be asleep, but when a knock sounded at my door, his head jerked up. Without thinking, I yanked open the door. Ezra looked deeply into my eyes as if she'd be able to see the pain in them.

"Hey, what's going on?"

Her eye-contact broke, and her gaze flitted to Finn. I looked over my shoulder and Finn made no efforts to cover himself. He smiled and waved proudly, donning his limp member like a participation trophy.

I sighed. "I was just—"

"It's okay," she said, taking my hands in hers.

She pulled me into the hallway and I looked around the abandoned area, curious.

"Are you okay? I sent everyone to their quarters while we get things sorted."

I swallowed a lump in my throat as the last hour replayed in my head in fast motion, ending with the Blood King triggering an orgasm. "I'll be fine."

She pulled me in for a hug and I wanted to wiggle free. I couldn't stand feeling so exposed. Every single person I knew was suddenly privy to my potential feelings, but if I panicked, I'd scare the shit out of Ezra.

I backed away slowly, making sure to keep my tone analytical. "So, we can't send the Hunters after him, right?"

Her gaze dropped and an expression I knew very well came over her face. She had looked the same when she'd asked me if I would choose to send the Hunters.

Guilt.

"What is it?"

She glanced around the deserted hallway. "I need to know if you can bear this."

"You mean, do nothing?" The words came out sharper than I meant them to.

She took me by the wrist and silently led me

through the tunnels to her chambers. The Hunters outside her door separated and let us through. She closed the door behind us.

Her voice was low. "I need you to be very honest with me."

I felt my emotions swell as tears threatened to spill from my eyes. "Okay," was all I managed.

I thought she was going to ask a question, but instead, she took a seat in a chair beside her bed. "Take your time. Tell me how you feel."

"Angry. Humiliated." I shook my head. "Disgusted."

"This is not your fault."

"How can you say that? My mate is a bloodthirsty murderer."

She pulled her knees to her chest. "He's hot, though."

"Fuck you."

She looked up at me slowly. Guilt swirled inside me. I shouldn't have taken any of this out on her. She was just trying to lighten the mood. Luckily, sister-hood proved to be durable. There was virtually nothing that I could do or say to truly damage it.

She walked over to me. I considered apologizing, but I didn't.

"What about the tether?"

You mean the ache in my chest that's fighting to find him? "If it's there, I want it cut."

She wrung her hands. "There's one way. The elders are putting pressure on me to push you into it, but I refused."

"What? Why would you do that? Ezra, I want this done."

"Because if things go wrong, I won't be able to save you."

"Just tell me."

She exhaled slowly before she spoke. "They want you to infiltrate the Blood Court as a spy and seduce the King."

I turned away, stunned, as my thoughts diverged into two paths. The first, born of the tether, was a powerful desire to meet the Blood King face to face. The second was the sudden realization that I was going to die. My mind shot through the stages of grief in a matter of seconds, before restarting. My immortality, they'd have me lose my immortality.

"All you'd have to do is make him fall in love with you, before you fall in love with him. Once you're sure his immortality is broken, you'll signal us. Our mages and Hunters will do the rest. The elders believe this is our opportunity to return to power.

We could topple the Blood Court if we play this right."

"I'm going to die."

"Not if you remember who he is. Not if you hold onto who you are. But say the word, and I'll fight the elders on this. We won't do it."

It was an impossible task. I don't think anyone had ever met their mate and lived longer than a mortal life afterward, and they were thinking about sending me directly to our enemy's court? There were only two ways I could see this going, and neither ended with me alive. Either they drained my blood immediately, discovering I couldn't die, torturing me for eternity. Or I'd trick them long enough to fall in love with my mate, and then when they drained me, I'd die. I didn't like those options.

"If he's my mate, how would I even stop myself from wanting him?"

She stood with her hands on her hips, watching me like our mother used to. "We could cast some protections, but it would ultimately come down to you. You'd need to find something stronger than the tether. Something you want more. I wasn't even going to ask, but you seemed so detached that I thought maybe the tether wasn't that strong."

If only she knew about that imaginary rendezvous. *No*. I'm definitely going to die. "I can't."

"Right," she said quickly. "Of course." She smiled. "You don't give this another thought. Your big sister is going to handle this."

I bowed icily and headed back to my room. I hated to disappoint her, but almost seemed relieved by my decision. My bedroom was empty when I got there, and I figured Finn had rushed off to meet up with the other Hunters.

How long had I dreamed of leaving these caves? How long had I wanted to become a Hunter? Ezra's mission would grant me both, but the cost was far too high.

I was glad for the opportunity to be left alone with my thoughts, but once I lay down and the world became quiet, I realized that until this was over, I would never truly be alone. I was bound to the tether. Tied 'til death to an immortal monster.

NINE

————— M A D D O X —————

*P*eng's fist slammed down on the table, and I snickered in response.

"Our army can't grow if you never allow anyone to join our court. They're mortals; of course they're imperfect. You can't be so selective."

I yawned. "Believe me, if I'd been King when you were presented to this Clan, you wouldn't have made the cut."

A chortle burst from Aiko, and she covered it with a fake coughing fit.

I propped my elbows on the table and rested my head in my hands.

"Sire," someone said from across the room. "You should take this more seriously."

Irritation burned hot in my throat, but I exhaled it and leaned back in my chair. "Ignorance is rampant in our court." I pulled my hair back securing it with a band. The bottom strands were too short to stay and I felt the tickle of them as they slipped out and came to rest at the back of my neck. I stood, slowly walking toward the front door. I stopped when I got midway across the room and turned back to the table and eyed each member of the clan. "You'd imbue all mortals if you got the chance."

Peng said, "If we did, we could wipe out the other courts."

"And to what end? The Blood Court is already the highest court. Greed will be our undoing."

Another Clan member chimed in. "Are we to understand that you never intend on exterminating the other courts?"

Peng grinned. "He's leaving us open to attack. If we don't bolster our numbers, the other courts will catch up and the courtiers agree."

I sighed. "Your lack of understanding astounds me." I was met with a row of blank stares. *This is why you don't grant immortality to whoever presents a decent case.* "Each mortal who turns is one less to feed on and one more to feed. The courtiers depend on us to supply them with sustenance as does everyone in this room. You've been provided for for far too long and don't remember how it feels to be thirsty. You seek power and plot against me, riling the spoiled courtiers into rebellion-- waiting for a moment to take my throne--completely oblivious to the fact that you're marching your own court to extinction," I scoffed. "You'd invite unworthy scum into our court for all of eternity without a second thought, yet you claim that I'm the one who isn't taking the task seriously." I smiled and headed toward the door, but said over my shoulder, "If you go looking for trouble, you'll find it. Just ask my father."

I only made it halfway to my chamber when Ronan found me. "I heard what happened."

"I'm not in the mood for a lecture."

"I agree with what you said."

My ears pricked.

"Increasing our numbers too quickly and thoughtlessly will most certainly lead to a loss of power."

I nodded to the guards outside my quarters and they opened the doors. I moved to make my escape, but Ronan followed me.

"Just spit it out."

He tugged at his collar nervously and I caught a glimpse of a scar.

"Sire, nothing good is going to come from alienating the rest of your court."

"How did you get that scar?" I asked.

He slipped two fingers under his collar as if he could feel the memory in its rigid edges, and his voice came out softly. "War."

"No shit."

He moved over to the couches and had a seat, as if in preparation for a long story. I felt a flare of excitement as I went to the bench on my windowsill where I did my best processing.

"It was one of the last days of the war. The Shadow Mages had already been wiped out, the Shifters were on their last legs and the Fae were the last real threat left fighting. I was in tough shape after taking an arrow to the shoulder. My vision blurred, and my immortality strained against the arrow's venom. I stumbled back toward our base, but a small pack of Shifters caught me out alone and chased past the tree line. I was outnumbered, exhausted, and sure they'd scatter my limbs and use them for chew toys for eternity."

I would have given anything to participate in the war, but I wasn't yet of age, and my immortality hadn't fully set in. The members of my court who had participated or thrived, carried an unspoken badge of honor that I could not wear. It held enough weight that even those below my rank could question my decisions—a king eclipsed by his own soldiers—I didn't know our enemies like they did. I'd never witnessed the unique carnage of each immortal element in its rawest form.

Ronan turned to the window as he continued. "The disgusting beasts growled, and I saw in their beady eyes that they still thought they had a chance, they still thought themselves better than the Blood Court. I was overtaken with rage, and I put those mutts down one by one. Their fight dimmed with each ally lost. I stood victorious over twitching limbs."

I nodded with the assumption that he'd reached the end. The tale was entertaining enough, but didn't answer the question at the back of my mind. Why hadn't his immortality healed him? Vampires, Shifters, and Fae had gotten into small skirmishes since my reign--but as far as I knew, none yielded scars, or at least, none that couldn't be healed with immortality over time. But before I could ask, Ronan continued.

"I was badly injured, claw and teeth marks reached down to my bones. My consciousness dimmed as I stumbled for the tree line. Just as I made it to the light, I fell, and my shadow stretched out in front of me."

Shadow Mage.

"A figure rose from the darkness, muttering an enchantment that engulfed her hands in darkness. She reached out for me." When his gaze moved to me I saw a flicker of fire in them. "That's the last thing I remember."

"My father had slew her, the last Shadow Mage."

He stood. "He saved my life, but I wasn't able to save him. His legacy as a Shadow Mage killer lives on. They were a great threat, even to themselves."

He headed for the door, but I needed no more information. Shadow Mages had always sounded powerful in stories, but if the bulk of their court had died of old age from divining their mates, they were hardly worthy of their power.

TEN

J jolted awake as someone burst through my door. Finn stormed in, glaring at me.

He didn't bother closing the door behind him, but another Hunter poked her head in and said, "Make it fast," before closing the doors.

I groaned. "Aren't you all supposed to be guarding me?"

Finn's expression was rigid and determined as he stormed to my bedside. He was usually so easy-going. I'd never seen him look so severe, but as a Hunter, I knew he must have a killer instinct somewhere inside. I just never expected him to turn it on me, his Princess. I eyed my clock; it was 8:00AM.

His words cut like knives. "What the hell is wrong with you?"

I slid out of bed and stood, annoyed that I wasn't a few inches taller. "Excuse me, *servant*?"

"Ferah is threatening to overthrow your sister, and you're just going to let her do it?"

I'd barely woken up, and he had the audacity to not only drop that bomb, but to blame me for it?

"What are you talking about?"

There was no way Ferah would do something so treasonous.

"If you can't stoop to care about the Shadow Court or your sister, do it for you."

"Do what? March to my death?" *How dare he?* I was so angry I could barely pull together responses without spitting.

"You're immortal."

"Not if I fall in love with him."

"Then don't."

I crossed my arms, but when his gaze flickered to the gesture I threw my arms out and shoved him. "You have no business attacking me like this. You know it won't be as simple as 'Don't do it.' He's a killer. He eats people."

"You're scared. I get that, but there's too much on the line here, Sin."

The mention of my name disarmed me.

Finn's voice softened. "You wanted to be a

Hunter? This is your chance. Hunters don't choose their missions, taking whichever ones sound safest."

I tried to respond, but the words got lodged in my throat.

"I know you, Sin. You're not going to let them overthrow your sister."

Inside I was screaming, as flashes of fangs cutting into my flesh dashed across my imagination. Finn walked towards me, his expression softening. He rubbed my arms, and I pulled away.

"I could come with you. Be your shadow."

Is he insane? If they discovered him, we'd both be killed. "That's twice as dangerous."

"And yet, still worth the risk. Our court doesn't belong underground," he said, his gaze burning into me. "The bigger the light, the stronger the shadow. If you make him mortal and kill him, you'll be the greatest Hunter that ever lived."

"Don't try and play on my ego. That won't work."

"Really? Because you look terrified and I think it's because you've already made up your mind."

I paused, then let out an exhale of surrender. "Where is she?"

"The Queen? She's at the drop with Ferah and the other elders."

I chewed on my bottom lip. "Leave, I need to change before I go."

"It's nothing I haven't seen before," he said, his excitement over his victory slipping into his voice.

"I said, get out."

A few minutes later I readied myself and swung my doors open, but Finn wasn't there. I forgot I'd sent him away. Now I needed him to come along if not for emotional support, for the simple fact that I was going to pitch him as my shadow for the mission. But I understood his reluctance. Ferah was the leader of the Hunters and his direct superior. The tension between Ferah and my sister was not one he could get in the middle of, but I could.

There was no way to mentally prepare for what I was about to do, and worse, I doubted Ezra would let me take such a risk on her behalf. However, Finn had been right about one thing: this was my only chance to become a Hunter.

The Hunters parted, allowing me passage onto the top of the granite spiral staircase which stretched around the drop. I could see my sister on the center platform, standing with her head held high and her crown glimmering with darkness. On the far side of the platform, Ferah stood with several of the elders, huddled in a semi-circle as they whispered to each other.

My shoes scraped the ground, echoing down the drop into the seemingly endless pit. I compiled my list of demands, as I wanted to do it on my terms. I wanted as many protections as I could get. Finn would be my shadow, and I wanted an official position as a Hunter. But most of all, I wanted to be the one to take the Blood King's life.

I made my way down, but quieted my steps to listen as Ferah turned away from the elders to my sister. Ferah's movements and appearance were smooth and pointed like a snake, as was her unpleasant demeanor, but her killer instinct when backed into a corner had turned our broken survivors into formidable Hunters.

She hissed. "You've let your personal feelings cloud your judgement on what's best for our people."

My sister held her ground. "I won't make her do it and what you're preparing to do is treason. I was the one who took away the choice and revived this court."

"And you will see it destroyed as well. You are unfit to lead us."

Something in me snapped. Who the hell did she

think she was speaking to her Queen like that? Ezra had banned execution to bolster our numbers, but this was the first time I'd seen a lack of respect from any of our subjects, even since then. Finn was right, this was serious, but I had the power, and thanks to Ferah's little outburst, my terms shifted.

"Enough," I called as I made my final descent to the highest platform. All six women watched me expectantly, except for Ezra, whose concern was marked by a wrinkle between her brows. "I will accept the mission, but I have conditions."

The elders, who looked no older than twenty mortal years, immediately brightened and Ferah bowed her head respectfully.

"A wise decision," Ferah said. "I'm sure we can accommodate your terms. Please," she said, gesturing for me to come closer, "Name your terms."

My sister interjected. "You don't have to do this." Ferah's face tightened and I could practically hear her tail rattling.

I held my hands out, palm down. "I've made my choice."

"Excellent," Ferah said. "Now, the terms."

"I shall be granted all resistance protections from our best casters."

"Of course, your Highness," Ferah said with a smile.

"I shall select a Hunter to shadow me for the duration of my mission."

Ferah straightened. "Lerant is skilled enough to—"

"I want Finn."

She threaded her fingers together. "Perhaps someone with more experience?"

"I want Finn."

She bowed her head. "As you wish."

I could feel my sister's gaze burning into the side of my face.

"I want to kill the Blood King myself."

Ferah slithered toward me, her eyes black slits through glassy yellow bulbs. She forced a laugh. "When an opportunity arises, you may make the first attempt on his life. However, if you should fail, my Hunter will finish the job. Sound fair?"

I grinned wickedly, my gaze shifting to my sister for a fraction of a moment before I delivered my finishing blow. "Funny you should mention, 'your Hunters' because that's my final request."

Ferah raised an eyebrow.

"On the completion of this mission I will be

granted your position as the Head Hunter and you'll be demoted to my underling."

She looked amused. "You?"

"Those are my terms."

"Impossible, but I might consider making you a Hunter."

"I was going to ask for that, but then I saw how you disrespected your Queen. I think you need to be reminded who you serve."

Ferah's voice was casual but her gaze shifted nervously to the four elders. "The elders will never agree to this."

Instead of their confirmation, their judgmental gazes sent Ferah coiling into a panic, her movements twitchy and her eyes unblinking.

Time to finish her. "Sounds like you've let your personal feelings get in the way of what's best for our people."

ELEVEN

*T*he greenhouse sprouted to life, with fronds reaching out as I passed a row of potted Geraniums. The air was wet and fragrant with mist teeming off the waterfall, and filling the garden with thick cloud-like plumes just below the top of the hundred and twenty foot glass ceilings.

I circled the mossy mountain structure at the center, climbing the staggered floor plates that wrapped around the internal core. I closed my eyes to listen more closely to the hum of the garden. My ears twitched and I rounded the corner where a spore drooped. The bulb weighed on its delicate stem, split, and threatened to snap. I knelt and touched a hand to the spongy wall and felt its life energy flicker weakly within the vibrant web of life. I touched it gently, bowing my head and sending my life force, first to my fingers, then to the wounded stem. The sound of footsteps approaching disrupted the bridge, but I forced more energy into the struggling plant. It straightened, its cells thickening and its bulb lifting until it was secure once again against the wall.

A man cleared his throat. "King Delton, you have a visitor."

I stood, drinking in my Chamberlain. He was pristine as ever, the medallions on his armor freshly shined, the greenery woven through his hair secure, his eyes rested and alert, but his stiff posture and the way his fingers twitched warned me that something was amiss. "Cadmus, you look unwell."

"I am perfectly well, your Highness, but you have a visitor."

"I will see them when I have finished tending to the greenhouse."

I turned away, prepared to resume my work when I felt Cadmus' energy shift. It rose in intensity, but instead of peace and balance, I felt twinges of apprehension and fear.

I turned. "What is it, Cadmus?"

His nostrils flared and he tucked a loose strand of icy-white hair behind his pointed ear. "There's a woman here, your Highness. I think you'll want to meet her."

A vague answer from the most direct person I knew meant he wasn't sure of what we were dealing with yet. He only withheld information when he wasn't certain of the truth. I followed him to my throne room, as the canopy spilled light onto the potted foliage at the base of the Redwoods. The mother tree separated her branches, revealing my vine-woven throne. Mother tree rustled as if in an indistinguishable breeze and in the hush of it, I felt her calming presence calling out in support.

I nodded to Cadmus and he signaled the Obstinacy at the door. The doors opened and several Obstinacies marched in with their bows, slung over their shoulders. I could feel the dark energy sapping away the greenery behind them. A buck lowered its horns. *What is this?*

The Obstinacy split and, reverting to tradition, took a knee beside the stranger. I observed the woman that scowled up at me, too intrigued to have her thrown out until I had confirmation of what I already suspected. Why come to the Arrow Court alone, and with ill intent? Her brow furrowed. It wasn't a scowl on her marble-like face, but she merely squinted at the errant beams of light that forced their way through the trees. She had the poised elegance of royalty, the calm nature of an assassin, and such levels of beauty that I hadn't seen in so long, I thought I'd imagined it all. Even her dark, dusty cloak didn't give her away, yet my mind wrestled with the improbability.

Impossible.

"Speak!" I demanded, impatiently. "Why have you come here?"

She blinked against the light, her discomfort as seemingly uncomfortable as it was to watch.

"Step closer," I said, gesturing to the bottom of my throne.

The limbs of the mother tree moved to block the light and the woman stepped forward, and her piercing gaze met mine for the first time.

My breath caught. "Shadow demon, why have you crawled from your shame? To throw yourself at our mercy?

"The shame belongs to all defeated parties, your Highness."

Heat flashed across my neck and the hall filled with the rustle of the trees, sensing my unease.

"Begone. Or I shall squash you and any other roaches from your court."

"I am the lone survivor. I hold no ill will to you or your court."

I clenched my jaw. *Nothing good can come of this.* "Then why have you come?"

She crossed her hands behind her back and a small smile moved onto her face. "The extinction of my court had much to do with our own weakness. Our nature was our undoing. I suppose war is also a part of nature, sussing out the dominant court to reign above the rest."

My grip on the armrests of my throne tightened, and I felt the bark threaten to give way beneath my nails. Vampires were a disgusting prideful breed, unworthy of their position. They used no logic, no sense, just brute force and hubris. They were no more fit to rule the immortals than the dogs of the Moon Court who now cowed to their every whim.

A wave of energy pulsed through my arms from the mother tree, a warning.

"Leave my court, witch, or you'll learn firsthand what a Fae Obstinacy's arrow tastes like."

Out of the corner of my eye, I could see Cadmus' body relax.

"I will take the arrow if you do not accept the gift I have prepared for you."

I raised my fingertips and the Obstinacies each knocked their arrows and aimed at the dark mage.

"Are you certain?"

She smiled and the only trace of fear that I felt in the room's energy web was my own.

I nodded.

"Since the extinction of my Court, I've longed for companionship, desperate to share my time with another. In my despair, I disregarded the dangers of my heritage and attempted to divine my mate."

A veil of unease settled through the room and the woman paused to savor it. We dared not speak of such dangerous things in the Arrow Court, and our attention was irrevocably arrested. Finally the mage spoke again, "I was unable to locate my mate and instead divined something with the power to defy nature. I found the mate of a king."

My eyes widened, fear pulsing into my body, as my life slipped into her hands. *My mate?*

Cadmus yanked the bow off his shoulder and rushed the yellow-eyed woman, pressing the tip of his arrow to her cheek. "How dare you bring such information here!" he shouted and the mage leaned away from the arrow. "I will not allow you to reveal it and risk the life of the Fae King."

I was frozen, terrified that if I spoke, I might

disagree. That curiosity would pull me to my demise and put my entire court at risk. But even with Cadmus' poisonous arrow pressed to the mage's cheek, she showed no sign of fear. Her gaze met mine with pleased resolve.

Her lips parted.

"Say one word and you die."

"Cadmus!" The name shot out like a reflex. "Let her speak."

Cadmus backed away slowly and a bright smile slipped onto the stranger's face. "I assure you, I mean you no harm. The king I was referring to was King Maddox of the Blood Court."

Silence fell on the room like a thick fog and we each breathed in the toxic temptations of our own devices. Just when I thought it wouldn't end, Cadmus broke it. "What is your name?"

Her gaze slithered to me as she said, "Ferah."

Finding my voice, I stood and descended the stairs to meet her at the bottom of my throne. "And what is it that you ask in exchange for such intriguing information?"

"I wish to serve you, your Highness. I wish for refuge in your court."

TWELVE

*E*zra chewed her thumb nail as we waited for Ferah's signal, but she looked less like a queen and more like a worried older sister. I leaned back in Ezra's granite throne, my own thoughts occupied by my imminent demise.

I felt the tug of Finn moving inside my shadow like a puppet on strings, but I swallowed the urge to lean in the opposite direction to counterbalance it. It was not the glamorous Hunter training I'd longed for all of my life. Not the furious lethal strikes nor the weeklong rock climbing courses over the dark empty pits. I need only to be still and ignore Finn's presence as I would when I stood before the Vampire King. If I let any indication that Finn hid within my shadow we'd surely be dismembered and tortured for all eternity.

But even that would have been favorable compared to the alternative. If I somehow allowed myself to be seduced by the Blood King, my immortality would wane and I'd throw away my infinite birthright, expose my court, and likely lead them all to extinction. Those fears were evident in Ezra's distant gaze but when she finally spoke, her words surprised me.

"Do you think Ferah will betray us?"

"I don't. And neither do you. She may have wanted the throne but only with the intent to lift our court."

She shook her head. "You didn't have to antagonize her with your conditions."

I shrugged. "Didn't I?"

Finn yanked at my shadow and I bit back a smile. His form sprung from darkness, a thick black cloud that dissipated into a Hunter. "You smiled. You can't do that," he said flatly.

"People smile, you know. Sometimes for no reason."

Ezra spun to us. "You're not taking this seriously. Are you not worried what that monster is going to do to you?"

Her glare was hateful, but behind it was only

concern for my safety. I swallowed a lump in my throat. She was overruled, even by me, tossing her only family into the heart of the enemy for the sake of our Court. If the roles were reversed, I doubted I could have done the same, but it was that deficit of character that made the subjects in our court glad that she was first in line.

"You are not forcing this task on me. This is what I want. The choice has been made."

As I spoke, I realized this was not so different from the choice Ezra had worked so hard to eliminate, only I had every intention of being my own Hunter, regardless of if Finn seemed to think he'd be the one to take the Vampire King's life.

She eyed me, her voice lowering to a pained whisper. "I wish I could take your place."

"I'm stronger than you think. I'll come back a hero. You'll make me a Hunter yet."

She smiled, but it didn't reach her eyes. "As long as you come back safely, we'll sort out the rest."

Finn's voice broke our attention. "Have the enchantments settled in yet? We should get moving to the surface soon."

"I don't know what they're supposed to feel like." It was alarming how much of our plan relied on

Ferah and Ezra was right to doubt her, but only in the confines of our own court. At the end of the day Ferah was a member of the Shadow Court, and her allegiance was as tied to it as her immortality.

Before she left to convince the Arrow Court to offer me to the Blood King as tribute, she had cast enchantments on me. One spell accentuated my mortal features, but I had to avoid mirrors. There was also one that acted like a block on the tether, but when Ferah cast it, she warned me not to become reliant on it, because its effects would fade quickly over time.

But even with a ticking clock, I had many advantages. Civilizations were always toppled by the women in the shadows of history. In my vast experience with men, I'd come to know them as the greatly inferior sex. Easily manipulated, controlled, prideful, quick to anger, and often oblivious to the social currencies that women traded right in front of them. Not to mention fragile, hyper-sensitive, vulnerable, and emotionally stunted. And of all men who shared these traits, royal men had no equal for folly or ignorance.

Ezra watched me carefully, as if trying to read my thoughts. "I think you should alter your persona."

"No," Finn said. "She's his mate, she should act normally. Besides, our spies confirm the king prefers. . ." he looked me up and down, "confident women."

"She'll need to stand out. The tether should take away some of the work, but if she were chaste and innocent, she might stand out from the other tributes. She could even avoid being bitten or touched for a while."

Finn pressed his lips together to suppress a laugh. "Chaste? Sinna? No one is going to believe her."

I slapped him upside the back of the head. "Enough. I'm the Shadow Court's only hope at redemption, and none of you have a shred of faith in me."

"I'm sorry, Sin," Ezra said. "This is just a lot to process."

"Then let's be glad I'm the one who's taking it on."

The throne room lights dimmed, and we plummeted into total darkness for a few moments before they returned to their normal, dull glow.

My gaze locked with Ezra's. "That's Ferah. It's time."

I should have felt more apprehension, but one of

my dreams was so close. My head rushed with the whispered memories the Hunter's shared about the mortal world above. Finn and I would begin our trek to the surface where I'd hide among the living until King Delton came calling.

THIRTEEN
— M A D D O X —

*R*onan crossed his arms over his chest, and the soft glow of the blazing fire-place haloed his head.

"I don't think it's wise to leave the Blood Court, not while things are so tense with the council."

I narrowed my eyes. "I wasn't asking."

Embers popped in the fireplace behind him. I saw a flicker of the fire's light behind his brown eyes that hinted at his annoyance.

He leaned in. "Maddox, don't push them."

I exhaled through my nose. "Fine, I'll approve three of their choices for the Blood Court. Now accompany me to the town before I think better of it and bring along someone I actually like."

"It's a full moon, Sire."

"I won't hunt. I just need to get away from this place, and I wager you do, too."

His face brightened, and his features softened. "The pub then?"

"Where else?"

Ronan and I didn't agree on much, not about politics, not about how to rule the Blood Court, but we both appreciated a night at the local pub. Intoxication purged all manner of fascinating truths from the lips of otherwise dull mortals.

We bundled up. The autumn air was colder than normal for the season, or perhaps it felt that way since we had moved away from the fire, but I'd never had a night in the pub that wasn't unbearably sweaty and full of lush, red-cheeked patrons. Plumes of mist burst from my lips with each breath as Ronan and I made our way down the winding hills that sheltered the cathedral. The walk was a short fifteen minutes from the town, but it was the long, drunken trudge back up the steep pathway that I usually forgot to consider.

Compared to the cathedral, the rest of the town was plain and lacking in the refinements that come with a thousand years of generational wealth. It only functioned at a basic level, yet it had charming buildings, and cobblestone roads that discouraged travelers from driving through. In comparison, the cathedral which had once housed the worship of mortal gods, and now housed immortal demons, looked as out of place, and it truly was. I saw a jewel being swarmed by roaches. I supposed our wealth was one of the reasons why so many were eager to volunteer to join our court, even given the high risk. We paid a small sum to the governor to allow us to continue, with the understanding that we could only drain volunteers.

Of course, we didn't always follow that rule, but there was no breach that money couldn't easily resolve. Ronan's pace increased when we were close enough to hear laughter and could see the yellow light pouring from the pub's foggy windows. I bit back a laugh as he practically sprinted the last few feet. The cold bit at my knuckles as Ronan pulled open the door, and a wave of heat greeted us along with the thick and saliva-inducing scent of fresh blood. Ronan stopped in his tracks and turned to me, pausing before we entered the blood-scented building.

I had to admit it was much stronger than I remembered. Perhaps the cramped pub was more packed than usual, but there was nothing that enticed me more than a battle of wills. Ronan's teeth were still a little red from his last meal, so I was certain he'd be able to behave himself.

I nodded to him, and we began our unlikely search for an empty seat. I could feel stolen glances from the fifty or so mortals, but they all appeared to know better than to be caught staring outright. The bulk of them crowded around tables littered with glasses filled with pale hued liquids that ranged from clear to honey brown., but there were a fair few that were standing around the bar where an exhausted bartender rushed back and forth like he was on skates.

I grinned. These were not the polished beauties that Delton or Herod sent as tribute, though their thick, supple forms seemed more appetizing, and their boisterous, exuberant exclamations seemed more appealing. My appraisal of the crowd halted when I noticed two divine forms glaring at me from the corner. The wolfish blue gaze of King Herod, and the green-eyed pointy-eared King Delton.

A grin stretched onto my face as I patted Ronan on the back to get his attention over the noisy crowd. I nodded to the corner and we wove our way through the scattered tables. Herod lifted his cup and downed the remainder of his beer before standing. He was wearing a shirt for once, if the shredded material that was slung over his shoulder could even be considered a shirt. I was preparing to tease him about it, when I realized he was leaving.

Was he sore about our last interaction? "Leaving so soon?"

He bowed his head respectfully. "Afraid so."

I turned to Delton, but the Fae King seemed unfazed by my presence. His arms were slung lazily up on the top of his booth, and his drooped head and hollow eyes indicated that he'd had quite a few drinks already.

Ronan patted me on the back before taking Herod's seat. "Don't worry about it. It's me he hates."

Delton snorted. "You must be quite used to it by now."

I cleared my throat and Ronan jumped back up. "So sorry. Another round Delt?"

He nodded, and Ronan hustled back to the bar where the crowd immediately parted to let him through.

"I haven't seen you here in some time," I said. "Tending to your flowers?"

He smirked. "Something like that." He finished his beer. "I've heard you've been a shut in as well. That council of yours not giving you trouble?"

I glared at him and Ronan placed three beers

between us. "Gentlemen, let's not waste a perfectly good night at the pub on politics."

We raised our glasses and toasted the pub, not as immortals but as three men looking for a bit of amusement. By the thirteenth drink, we each had a woman or two on our laps entertaining us with offers of the eternal sexual favors they'd provide if we made them immortal. My vision blurred, but I'd been swept up in the euphoric energy of the night. I was thoroughly enjoying the alcohol-induced bond between Delton, Ronan, and me, even if it would only last until the ale stopped flowing.

FOURTEEN

inn squeezed my hand in the dark as we climbed our way up the tunnels towards the surface. I knew the gesture was meant to ease any anxiety, but I refused to let that be the case. If the Vampire King was going to capture every waking thought once the tether grew stronger, I wanted to savor every second of sanity I had left. My thoughts were consumed with the surface. I'd dreamed of visiting for even longer than I'd wanted to be a Hunter. Although I'd seen it before we went underground, those memories had all been replaced with the dark and safe tunnels that made up my life. With each step of the long, ten-hour trek, the air felt colder and more pure, until I could feel the bite of winter nipping through my fur coat. Finn smirked.

"Why couldn't we have been sent on a lovely summertime mission?"

I stopped as a tiny whistling sound echoed through the caves.

"We're nearly there," Finn said, turning to face me. "You know the plan?"

I nodded.

"Then I'm going to shadow you. Assume there are spies from the other courts watching at all times, and don't acknowledge me, but," he said, brushing my chin, "remember. I'm with you always."

He leaned in but I turned my cheek to meet his lips. The corners of his mouth drooped a fraction before he began to melt into the floor, his body darkening into a charcoal black pool, before disappearing beneath my feet and blending with my barely visible shadow.

I didn't like the finality of a kiss. It felt too much like goodbye. This was a mission, plain and simple. Not only was I coming back, but I was coming back as a Hunter. A fraction of Finn's weight tugged at my shadow, and the already strenuous walk wore on my tired legs. I knew I'd have to acclimate to the added weight, and quickly, but after several minutes passed in dark silence, I missed Finn's conversation.

I was about to insist that he come out of shadow

form, at least until we got a little closer, but something in my peripheral vision caught my eye. A thin, crescent moon-shaped glow stretched across the rocky terrain in front of me, and a second brighter version of the same shape beamed on the edge of the cave. *This is it.* The added weight on my shadow was buried by my enthusiasm as I raced toward the light. I knelt, dipping my fingertips in the beams that spilled onto the floor of the tunnels, wishing there was a way to bottle the glow and keep it.

I followed the trail of light to the exit, the bite of winter entangled with the moon's light as I peered through the opening. I lay my hands flat on the bolder that blocked the path and pushed. It didn't budge, so I pressed my shoulder against it, lowered my stance and drove into it all of my weight. The massive stone didn't even stutter. I peered through the opening, my eyes clamping shut as the moon's light shot straight into my eyes. The other side was littered with snow covered trees that glistened with white moon dust.

What am I supposed to do? I'm too close to the surface to ask Finn, someone might hear and I can't shadow through the gap, without the risk of being seen. The crunch of footsteps in the snow outside the cave sent a chill through my body. I ducked away from the opening, putting my back to the stone and stifling my breaths. The crunching sound drew closer, then multiplied, until I could no longer detect how many mortals were on the other side. I swallowed a lump in my throat, my heart racing as I listened with keen interest.

A familiar voice floated through the gap. "I've imprisoned her here."

Ferah. I thought I'd have an hour or two to explore the mortal town before she was to come find me, but the trek to the surface must've taken us longer than expected. I peered through the gap, and the moonlight snuffed out. A green-eyed figure glared at me. His white hair practically glowed in the moonlight, his ageless face and beauty reeked of immortality and I wondered if my half-mortal blood would be enough to mask my own immortality. I was paralyzed under his stare until he moved away from the gap, and I was able to see how bulky his frame was. I wouldn't have thought it possible but he made Finn and the other Hunters look weak by comparison.

"If this is a trick, witch, you'll die first."

I couldn't see Ferah from my limited view, and I waited for the hiss of her quick witted response, but she said nothing.

"Cadmus," his voice boomed. "You and the other Obstinacies push from this side. And you three, arrows at the ready in case our guest is foolish enough to run."

Run? I scoffed. Arrogant of him to believe me to be intimidated. This must be King Delton of the Arrow Court. I'd sooner spit in his face than run. My shadow tugged slightly, snapping me from my intrigued analysis back to the plan we'd pored over again and again the last few days. While I might've wanted to stand up, to knock the Fae King down a peg, I was supposed to be a shy and vulnerable mortal girl. I sat on the ground and pulled my knees to my chest, suppressing the groan that threatened to burst out as I pretended to cower. I heard a grunt, and silver moonlight spilled onto the cave floor, drenching my shoulders as I peeked through my hair.

"Please don't hurt me," I whispered, as the King strode to my side. He took my arm and forced me to my feet and I fought to break eye contact. The stories of the Fae's beauty, which I assumed to be exaggerated, now hardly seemed to live up to reality at all. He took my chin and tilted his head to let the moonlight fall on my face. The seconds dragged for so long as his gaze skimmed over my face, that I wondered if my cover was blown. Another Fae grabbed his shoulder snapping him from his thoughts. He dropped my chin and turned to his companion.

"Is it true?" the man asked. "Is this really the one?"

King Delton's eyes narrowed. "I'm not sure."

FIFTEEN

A gentle breeze sent white flakes drifting into the rocky cave as I observed the girl. Her teeth chattered and she bundled her fur coat tighter, staring at me with her honey-brown eyes. I was startled by the soft lines of her features. As I studied her, I saw that the moonlight lit up the golden tones within her skin, highlighting her lightly freckled cheeks. She was beautiful enough to halt me in a crowded street, and nothing less would have convinced me that she was in fact, the Blood King's mate, but it still didn't feel right. She was not the smoldering temptress that Maddox preferred, but a terrified and fragile blossom, wilting from being held too close to my immortal sun. She was far more suited for me than him. It was that thought that struck me motionless as I lost myself in the ocean of her tear-filled eyes..

My curiosity and imagination had been working full time to create an image of Maddox's mate from the moment I agreed to this plan, but I had greatly missed the mark. I had expected to meet the woman who would topple the Blood Court. I'd expected this to be an easy task. I'd gleefully ship her off to the blood drinkers where she no doubt belonged, but the shivering doe-like woman stirred my empathy.

Cadmus' voice broke my trance. "Let's get her out of the cold."

I turned and left her to my Obstinacies as I breathed in the serenity of the frozen forest. Ferah made her way to me, her dark eyebrow raised, and her mouth twisted into a pleased smile. "Well?" she said, her gaze sweeping over my face.

"We shall see."

A slight movement in the corner of my eye made my ears twitch, but the snow-white terrain remained unblemished. "Stay with the Obstinacy. I'll be right back."

I walked through the forest and closed my eyes, focusing on the hushed whispers of the woods. I tuned out the Obstinacies as they began to march the girl back to the greenhouse and the creak of the trees as they pushed against the wind. Then I heard the sound I was listening for, the sound of retreating waves that rose and crashed on the shore. The steady unmistakable rhythm of wolfish lungs. I opened my eyes, and several snow-white masses rose from the snow. Their beady eyes glared and the white of their canine teeth shone in the wintery moonlight.

I held my ground as one of the wolves began to shift. I always hated being present for a shift. It was an unnatural abomination of snapping ligaments and bone as the snow-white wolf morphed into a man. I cleared my throat. "Herod."

His chest was covered in blue markings as he began to circle me, like he forgot he was no longer in wolf form. "What's going on here?"

"I need you and your mutts to leave now."

A wolf growled and snapped at the air beside me.

Herod smiled brightly. "I'm not leaving shit."

The last thing we needed was to draw more attention to what we were doing. I nodded to the wolves at his side. "Call them off, and I'll tell you."

Herod crossed his arms and glared at me. Finally, he nodded, and without a word the wolves headed back through the woods.

"Now," he said, "tell me what's going on here."

I looked around the empty forest, heard the retreating footsteps of the Obstinacies in the deep snow, the girl, and the wolves as they raced through the dense forest.

"I found Maddox's mate."

He studied my face. "You seem very certain of that."

"I had a lead and I wanted to check it out before I came to you."

"And?"

"It's her."

He nodded but his muted reaction suggested he wasn't convinced. "I'd like to see her for myself."

"You're putting us more at risk by being here."

His breath released a cloud of dewy, white air. "You expect me to believe you without proof?"

"Tomorrow I will present the girl to Maddox along with other tributes. If he keeps her around, you'll have your proof, but I suggest you prepare for a battle. Once the King's immortality is compromised, we will only have a small window to take him down, and the rest of his court won't go down easily."

His nose twitched. "This doesn't smell right. What aren't you telling me?"

I'd hoped to keep my deal with Ferah a secret, but Herod was right to question this. Outside of the Shadow Court, there was no way to find an immortal's mate aside from dumb luck. Herod was always suspicious, and he certainly wasn't going to like how we'd ended up in business with Ferah.

"We kept a prisoner from the war. A shade. She agreed to divine Maddox's mate and retrieve her, in exchange for sanctuary in our court."

Herod's blue eyes lit as my story began to take root in his head.

"I want to see the girl."

"In due time," I said, looking over my shoulder. "Don't you think it'll raise suspicions for Mad if she knows us both? Give it some time, visit the Blood King and if she is what we think, I'm sure he will be eager to show her off."

With a twitch of his nose, he turned away, his body contorting as the white, wolfish fur pierced his skin like tiny needles through dark brown fabric. I hurried after the Obstinacies and their mysterious prisoner. If we were going to use her to catch Maddox's eye, she'd need a lot of work before I presented her to the Blood Court tomorrow morning.

SIXTEEN

 W e trudged through the snowy terrain, the crunch of the snow beneath my boots was unfamiliar in the way my foot sunk into it. The air was crisp and dry, as the Fae King's Obstinacies marched me through the woods. Each court had their own version of Hunters, the military force that kept them in power. I had to admit that the Obstinacy was pretty cool with their pointed ears and earthy uniforms. I had hoped they'd take me through the town, so that I could glimpse the warm buildings, all nestled together, and perhaps the mortal faces that reminded me of my mother, but the Fae stayed in the woods, unwilling to risk me being seen by The Blood King until I was ready to be presented. The moonlight glittered over the unmarred snow like luminescent crystals. Winter was shaping up to be my favorite season. Finn had described the season as a barren wasteland, but all I saw in the shimmering branches was a crystalline wonderland.

Those who favor warm climates are foolish. I'd no sooner thought the words when I caught my first glimpse of the Fae Greenhouse, stretching up above the tree-line. It was a lush, tropical world, green and vast, trapped behind foggy windows. It was obstinate both in its grand dome-like structure and defiance of the season, like a reverse snow globe. The vibrant greens pressed against the glass panes, beckoning us out of the cold, as the strange sight rose from the forest like a mirage in the desert.

My steps became labored. There was a weight pressing in on my chest, harder with each step. I couldn't possibly be fatigued already. I lifted my hand and placed it on my chest, and my heart raced against it. Each step farther from the caves drained my energy, like this world knew I didn't belong. But why? My legs felt strong, my lungs were unencumbered from the journey, unless... was it the tether? I let my gaze wander until it came to rest on an unremarkable section of the woods.

"Are you alright?" King Delton asked, tearing me from my reverie.

This was no time to show my hand. "I need to rest," I muttered.

He gestured to the dome-shaped greenhouse. "We're nearly there."

I nodded, but his gaze moved to the direction I'd traced the tether and his wild, green eyes narrowed. He moved ahead of me, the fletching and nock of his arrow peeking out over the top of his quiver, but they didn't jostle, not even with the Fae King's powerful and uneven gate. Ezra had told me of the powerful poisons that tipped all arrows of the Fae. If the stories were true, they couldn't be handled lightly, so it shouldn't have surprised me that the quivers had a system to lock arrows in place. My curiosity began to take hold as I wondered about the intricacies of the other courts. We all lived so differently.

I'd been in their company for such a short time, but it was hard not to be seduced by the beauty of the Fae, and certainly the grace and nuances of their chosen method of killing. I was drawn to the idea of poison more than I cared to admit, and I hoped I'd get a chance to see it before they shipped me off to the blood court.

Up close the greenhouse looked like the emeralds that sometimes glittered along the walls of my home.

The green of the plants inside shone through the glass panes, which scattered the moonlight like a large gemstone atop the snow.

An Obstinacy opened the door and I held my breath in anticipation as the other Fae, and Ferah, herded me through the doors. A blanket of warmth and moisture clung to my face, and my extremities tingled from the change in temperature. The room was a jungle, with trees and vegetation sprawling across all but a narrow path that wove throughout it. The air was filled with the rustle and chatter of life hidden in the greenery, and I strained to catch a glimpse of whatever hidden creatures peered at us as we passed through the moonlit forest.

The path opened up, and at the far end of the room was a wooden throne carved into a massive tree. A deer froze as its eyes met mine, before it skidded into the depths of the forest. With the Obstinacy lined up, their bows at the ready, with arrows still secure in their quivers, it was easier to see their similarities and differences. Their facial features were kissed with the versatility of nature, but they all had the same shade of snow-white hair, and the same long pointed ears. I drank in the strange atmosphere, more certain than ever that if I had my choice of courts, I would have had no difficulty choosing the Arrow Court.

I was sure it wasn't only because I was experiencing something new. Anyone would have felt the same way. The essence of nature lives in all of us. Ferah slid into my field of vision across the room. As planned, she'd kept her distance, unwilling to give away our previous connection, and only now was her usual grimace replaced with a pleased smirk. My gaze moved to King Delton, whose eyes watched me with a softened gaze and a raised eyebrow. My wonderment was unintentional, but I could see how that might stroke the ego of an immortal king.

"Your Majesty," an Obstinacy said, "time is short."

The King's gaze dropped away. He flicked his wrist, a gesture I didn't understand, and two of the female Obstinacies, took me by the arms and led me out of the throne room. The rest of the manor was what I'd expected of the Fae court. It was elegant, if not a little plain. The corridors were made up of wood and stone, with small waterfalls trickling into black pools that reminded me of home.

"Where are you taking me?"

The Obstinacies exchanged a glance, a wordless deliberation on whether to respond, but ultimately they held their silence, choosing instead to nod toward a wooden door. Not wanting to appear too eager, I slowed my pace as I approached, looking back at the Obstinacies as they watched to make sure I'd enter. I pulled on the door handle and needed to use my body weight to yank it open. Thick white plumes of mist poured through the opening, and I peered through to the glimmering pools. A Fae woman approached me, nude as the day she was born, with her long silvery hair tucked behind her pointed ears.

The basins were rocky and similar in shape to what we used in the Shadow Court. In fact, there were more similarities than differences. It wasn't uncommon for our washers to be naked, but I'd known them all of my life.

The Fae woman reached for me, and I instinctively drew back.

"I'm Ava. I need to get you clean and to bed with the rest of the tributes."

Her gaze was soft, but her voice was full of urgency. I nodded and she carefully stripped off my clothing, took my hand, and led me down to the water. The black soot from the caves where I'd spent all my life was practically a second skin, but the woman scrubbed it until the rich brown color of my natural skin tone showed through.

The woman worked quickly and thoroughly, and I admired her beauty, both the ethereal lines of her profile, and the sheen of her glossy hair as it floated on the surface of the water. The corners of her mouth tipped up and I felt scorched by her green eyes as they flitted to me for the smallest moment.

"Are you not allowed to speak with me?"

She rose from the water, the translucent beads slipping down her torso as she ascended the stairs.

"Am I not allowed to speak with you?" I pushed as she disappeared into the mist, returning a moment later with a bottle.

"If you wish," she said softly.

She poured the bottle rather than squeezed it and when she placed it on a stone, I realized it was made of glass. She rubbed her hands together, and bubbles oozed through her fingers.

She sunk back into the water, the floral aroma filling my nose and making my eyes roll back as I breathed it in. The woman's touch was stronger now, her fingers digging into my muscles as she rubbed the scented oils deep into my skin. She grew more bold, teasing at my nipples, her expression warming and her lips playfully pursed as my breath skipped.

I felt a tug on my shadow which lay just on the

surface of the water around my shoulder. *Finn.* I'd been so overwhelmed by the Arrow Court that I'd almost forgotten about him. Was he warning me of a danger I couldn't see? Then I felt my shadow slide down my back and shortly after the press of Finn's shadowy fingertips on my thighs as he pried them open. The Fae women's eyebrows rose, as heat burned my face. What was Finn doing? He was going to get us caught. The woman eased me back against the rock with a smile. "You're different," she said, teasing her fingers down my body.

Heat radiated up my neck as desire began to flare along with curiosity. "How so?"

"Most of the tributes are terrified on their last night. I've always wondered why they don't-" she slipped her fingers between my legs, "-relax and enjoy their last night, since most of them don't survive a day in the Blood Court."

I forced myself through the pleasure and her warning to keep my eyes open, to watch the beautiful Fae girl, as I knew this would be my last chance to experience intimacy with a Fae. I knew there was truth to the danger she spoke of, but my body couldn't hear it, not with the pleasure building as I writhed against the cold stone.

"You'll meet the others tonight," she said softly.

My body jolted with delight, the motion sending glitter through her eyes and eagerness to her touch. But the Fae girl didn't know that she and I were not alone, that my shadow's hands were practiced, relentless, and knew exactly where to touch me to make me forget she was even there.

SEVENTEEN

I heard the faint whispers of the other tributes lilting down the hallway as Ava led me toward my room. Exhaustion settled into my muscles from the brutal climb to the surface, after I had calmed down from the wonder of seeing the fabled Arrow Court with my own eyes. I'd imagined the mortal town above so many times, piecing together Finn's stories and adding in my own daydreams, but I hadn't even glimpsed it. Instead I was given the rarest of opportunities to see an immortal court outside my own, an honor that only the crown King or Queen could possibly hope for, unless of course they were hidden away underground. Ava reached for the wooden door, and when it cracked open, the voices hushed.

I stepped through into a room that resembled a

grassy field. Moon and starlight beamed down through glass panes on the vaulted ceiling. Several women lay on blankets on the soft plane.

Ava gave me a moment to take in the splendorous view before returning with a blanket. "Big day tomorrow. Best get some rest, if you can."

I smiled my thanks and she closed the door behind her, locking it with a resounding click. I looked around at the motionless tributes, who appeared to be asleep, but I could practically feel their energy as I searched for an open place. I saw the first stirs of movement as curious eyes peeked at me through the dark.

I found an empty patch of grass between two women and lay down my blanket between them. I climbed onto it, surprised to find the blades of grass to be both soft and supportive beneath it. The day's physical and emotional weight threatened to pull me instantly to sleep, but I heard a faint voice whisper behind me.

"You're very beautiful."

I rolled to face the girl who had spoken. She peeked at me through glossy red hair. She had mortal eyes, just like my mother. The vibrant, hopeful eyes of someone who didn't know what would come next. I wondered if mine looked that way, now that I'd been thrust into new territory and would possibly face my own mortality in the near future.

"You're very beautiful, too," I said, remembering myself. "I'm Sinna."

"My name is Celine."

I offered a smile before I rolled onto my back. I didn't mind the conversation. It was a welcome distraction, and I'd been living off those since I had been given my mission. When I was idle, I felt over-whelmed by the tasks at hand. Don't get bitten. Stay in character. Seduce the King. Don't fall in love. I could feel the tension in the room, as if the other tributes were listening to my conversation with Celine, as if we were all clinging to the hope that tonight wouldn't be our last. I wanted to think the King would choose me and that my plan would go accordingly, but as I lay in the moonlight, I realized that every tribute there had that in common, and that like them, it could easily be me who died at the hands of the Vampire King.

I shuddered.

"Have you ever seen him?" Celine whispered.

My heartbeat stuttered as his pooled image rushed back. "No."

"My cousin saw him at the tavern once. She said

he was divinely beautiful. Can you believe it? *Divinely.* She said she'd die, just for the chance to be his immortal queen."

Existence seemed too great to give up for beauty, even divine beauty. I reminded myself that I wasn't here for beauty but for the elevation and protection of my family and court.

"Is there any beauty worth dying for?"

She paused so long that I wondered if she'd fallen asleep, then she said, "I hope so. She volunteered a few years back and never returned. I like to think it was worth it."

I sat up, my voice stronger than I meant it to be. "Then, why are you here?"

She sat up, sending her wild, red curls bouncing around her head. "Believe me. Any alternative to the life I've been born into is an improvement. . .Why are you here?"

My answer stalled on my tongue when I caught the smallest shift of my shadow under the moonlight.

I covered my face with my hands, finding it all too easy to force weakness into my voice. "I was taken."

Celine sucked in a breath.

"For fuck's sake," a voice boomed from behind

me. I turned to see a girl with strikingly angular features snarling at me. "Firstly, you're both going to die within three seconds of entering the Blood Court."

"That's needlessly harsh, Mel," someone whispered from across the room.

She pointed her finger past me. "She's too frumpy to catch the King's eye and the second you start with that hostage nonsense, the King is going to lose his shit."

I raised an eyebrow. "And I suppose you think he's going to choose you to be his bride?"

"We'll never know because if you half-wits chatter on all night like this, I'm going to off myself long before we get to the Blood Court."

A smile tugged at my mouth, and my next words were practically involuntary. "I like you."

She had no shame, played no games, and spoke her truth.

Her eyebrows rose, before her face fell back into a scowl. "Whatever. Go the hell to sleep."

Celine shrugged but her eyes glistened with a touch of sadness, no doubt wounded from Mel's harsh appraisal. I lay between them, intrigued by their uniqueness. By comparison, immortals seemed to eventually fall into the same few attitudes, never evolving into anything other than lustfulness, arrogance, and hunger for power. Celine was gentle, kind, and hopeful. Mel was strong, opinionated, and optimistic. Who was I?

The more words rose up to answer me, like deceitful, conniving, and promiscuous, the more they came to resemble the traits I'd assigned all immortals. If for the first time in my life my immortality was on the line, perhaps, I thought as I drifted off to sleep, I could be something else.

EIGHTEEN

I awoke suddenly. The sky was bright outside the skylight, but the sun was not yet high enough to shine through the misty glass panes. A line of Obstinacies marched with their pointed ears peeking through their hair. They stood at attention, crossing their bows as I and the rest of the tributes scrambled to our feet, brushing the sleep from our eyes.

Celine's gaze met mine, but in the morning light, her eyes were less hopeful than the night before, and instead, just beyond her neutral expression, there was a sheen of fearful despair. When I looked to Mel, her eyes were trained on the Fae Guards with the determined intensity that mirrored how I'd looked at the Hunters all my life.

The Obstinacies ushered us out of the meadow

atrium where we'd spent the night, through the cramped wooden labyrinth that appeared to make up the bulk of the Fae Court, until the room opened to a new, heavily wooded greenhouse. The branches of the canopy were woven together so tightly that there were only small slivers of space where the sunlight slipped through it, spilling silvery, white light through the candlelit greenhouse.

The other tributes took their seats in elegantly carved chairs that were set around a long wooden table at the center of the room. Celine stuck behind me like my shadow, but I thought I'd have to jockey for a position beside Mel. Surprisingly, instead of making her way right to the table, she lagged back a bit, wrapping her sleek ponytail around her finger as she over-intently examined her surroundings, losing interest just as I came up behind her. We wordlessly took a seat at the table as trays of thinly sliced fruit and multicolored rice were set out in front of us. As I looked around the table at the other girls, I could practically taste the anxiety in the air, or maybe it was my own. We were all going to face an excruciating death, and worse than that, we were all going to face him. A shudder tore through me as my mind brought forth the image of his dark, cold eyes.

When I looked up again, many of the girls had

already begun eating, some of the braver ones even chatting quietly on the far side of the table. I reached for my fork only to find the table completely without them. I eyed Mel, who smirked at me, giving a slight shrug of her shoulders before she popped a slice of yellow fruit into her mouth.

"How are we supposed to eat rice with our fingers?" I asked Celine.

Her curly red locks blocked most of her face, but her plate was already almost completely clear. I hadn't eaten in some time. Food wasn't necessary for my survival like it was for the mortals. It was more of a luxury. I reached for the rice, and to my surprise, it stuck together better than I'd anticipated and had a sweet buttery flavor.

When Celine finished her plate, she turned to me, her eyes moving to my plate ever so often as she made conversation. "You seem nervous today."

Her voice drew the attention of several of the other girls. I swallowed the rice I was chewing before I said, "I am."

"Are you more afraid to die, or that the Blood King won't choose you?"

I wasn't sure this was an appropriate breakfast conversation, but the rest of the tributes were listening intently now. I paused a moment to gather my thoughts. There was nothing about the situation that wasn't scary. If they discovered me, my whole court could be in danger. I could fail at my first task as a Hunter. What if the tether was too strong to resist? My neck stung as my mind played through the worst-case scenario.

The King biting into my neck.

If he did and I didn't bleed, my cover would be blown. Or worse, if he bit me and I did bleed, it would mean that I'd fallen in love with him and could no longer complete my task. Either way, I was sure being bitten was the worst. I couldn't reveal my other fears, but Celine and the rest of the girls would certainly buy this one.

"I'm afraid to be bitten."

There was a collective softening of the other girls as if the freely spoken words lifted some of their apprehension. Conversation swelled as the girls began sharing their hopes and fears.

"What about you, Celine?"

Her gaze moved to my plate before it snapped back to my eyeline. "I'm most afraid he won't love me."

Mel interjected. "What if you don't love him?"

A few of the girls giggled at that. Apparently, King Maddox didn't have the same reputation among the mortals. All my life, I'd heard nothing about the Blood Court other than their ruthlessness and cruelty.

Celine tripped over her words, so I took the opportunity to get to know a little about Mel. "Do you expect to fall in love with him?"

"I'm not here for love. I'm here for immortality. I don't have to be the King's true love. I just have to be interesting enough for him to want to keep me around."

I bit back a smile. *True love*. What an odd expression. Before I could inquire further, the Obstinacies barged in.

"Line up," one said, his voice echoing through the canopy.

I slid my plate to Celine, and with a few determined scoops, she polished it off, mouthing a 'Thank you,' before we were ushered into line with the others.

I was familiar with our next destination, the bathhouse. I was a little sad not to see the beautiful Fae girl from the night before, but instead, the Obstinacies stripped naked and stood in waist-deep water, ready to bathe us. Their steely bodies were beaded with water, as we were all ordered to strip and join them in the pools. None of us fussed much.

The beautiful immortal Fae had a way of numbing the senses. They were surprisingly thorough, swift, and business-like in their movements, as each tribute was washed and then rotated out to the next room. The Fae didn't offer so much as a salacious glance at any of the tributes. Even the more confident ones that had strut around in hopes of drawing their attention. It was as if they thought all mortals were inferior. Had my mother not been mortal, I wondered if I would have felt the same.

I was wiped down with a towel and sent nude through the hallway, where I was ushered to the next room. Some of the other girls were already there. Their wet hair was towel-wrapped on top of their heads like mine. The variation of skin tones, body types, and prominent features had me wondering if the King had any preference at all, but each girl had obvious beauty, even when stripped down and damp. Some of the girls were being measured, while others winced in the mirror as more Fae pulled their hair into styles that suited each girl, as if they were carefully planned and chosen.

The hours dragged. The activities were so tedious we could do nothing but fear the night ahead, and occasionally exchange those fears. When the first few girls slipped on their custom gowns, with white fabric cut flawlessly to complement their best features, they all could pass as immortals. It was odd to see the white fabric, so royal and elegant, but it was not worn by any of the courts. Arrow always wore green, Blood wore red, Moon wore blue, and the Shadow Court wore black. White felt like a blank slate, a statement of non-belonging. It wasn't until the Obstinacy zipped my dress as I caught a glimpse of myself in the mirror, that I felt naked for the first time. It was as if I no longer belonged to my court. My gaze trailed down the white fabric to my deep black shadow, and I felt the smallest bit of comfort. I was not alone. I was still a princess of the Shadow Court, and those were the thoughts I held onto all the way until I stepped foot in the Blood Court that night. After that, who I was, my mission, what I wanted, all slipped away from me like water through my fingers. After that, everything went to hell.

NINETEEN

MADDOX

J stood under the full moon, my breath coming out in white plumes, briefly obscuring the simmering orb, before dissipating. There was something about it that drew me out on clear nights. Perhaps it was the way it waned and eventually died, bright and temporary like the shooting stars that framed it. I envied them. The cold air quenched the burning thirst in my throat, and I reached out as if I could feel the beams of moonlight brush against my fingertips. Something was amiss, something I couldn't wrap my head around yet. I'd completely forgotten that Delton was presenting tributes tonight, but his footsteps behind brought the memory back to the surface.

"Sire, they're here."

A pang of sadness hit my stomach. I didn't want

to tear myself away from the moon's light and the peace that came with it, in exchange for a parade of women who would no doubt remind me of Nova.

"Sire?" Ronan said, his voice a little softer this time.

"Something is off," I said, turning to him. "Can you feel it?"

He pressed his lips together, and I could feel annoyance radiating from him, fueling me with a twinge of pleasure. It was enough to send me trudging through the cold, back to my stained glass prison. With every step toward the palace, my unease grew, until it felt like a weight resting on my chest. I could hear Ronan's footsteps behind me, so I squelched any visible signs of distress.

If this was something new, something that could shake me from the mundanity of eternal life, however abhorrent, it would be a welcomed change. When I stepped into the Blood Court, the sanguine aroma struck me so hard it could have knocked me off my feet. Instead, I went straight for the Throne room, where I knew the tributes would be waiting.

I pushed open the door as the weight on my chest threatened to crack my ribs. I pushed on to see Delton, sitting on the arm of my throne. Rage swelled, and I saw a glimmer of amusement in his swampy eyes.

I straightened and forced a smile. "If it isn't the King of the Fairies."

His jaw clenched as he stood. "It's Fae," he muttered.

"What do you have for me tonight?"

"A gesture of my respect and admiration of the Blood Court."

They were the same words as always, but tonight they had a bite to them that I couldn't place.

"Let's see them then," I said, walking down the small flight to the carpeted floor where the tributes waited to be appraised.

I strode past the first row, hardly glancing at the trembling tributes as I moved to the next row. When I stepped into the second row, the weight on my chest amplified. Was this a *tether*? My gaze moved to Delton whose mossy green eyes were locked on my every move. His eyebrow twitched, and a wave of shame slammed into me. Did he really think I'd be so easily killed? That I'd sacrifice my immortality for a sensation that literally felt like it was going to crack my ribs? It was simple; all I needed to do was walk by the tributes and order them all to be drained. I straightened and walked down the aisle, too afraid to look at the source of this feeling. I passed the tributes one by one until I could feel her beside me. My pace slowed, and my body refused to pass by. I forced myself forward but only made it a step before I stopped, my heartbeat throbbing in my chest. I turned to face the tribute standing next to the one with the tether, and promised myself to focus on her only. Her resemblance to Nova was uncanny. Dark straight hair, glossy blue eyes, and a stare that was equal parts cold and fearful.

"What's your name?"

"Melany," she said, but my focus was starting to drag away from her.

"Why are you here?"

"Immortality."

An honest answer, refreshing. I looked to Ronan, gesturing over my shoulder as words I never meant to speak slipped out. "I'll take these three. Have them in my chamber in an hour."

I turned to glare at Delton, who only bowed graciously and took his leave. Perhaps I'd given Delton too much credit. He didn't so much as snicker when I made my selection. I hadn't so much as looked at the girl, but that might've worked against me--feeding into my curiosity. If I would have looked, I was certain she wouldn't have been anything special, but it wasn't a risk I wanted to take so publicly.

I passed Ronan on my way out of the Throne room. "Drain the rest," I said, patting him on the back. "Let's eat."

I tried not to be preoccupied at dinner as I sipped fresh blood from the goblet, but my mind was occupied with what was waiting for me in my bed. Ronan seemed more at ease than usual, probably comforted that I had chosen three tributes instead of one, but the danger was greater than ever. I just needed to find out if it was greater than me. I took my time chatting with the other courtiers and some council members who all seemed in good spirits from our shared feast, and only when the numbers dwindled did I stand, and wish the straggling few a goodnight. I made my way to my chambers. I expected the intensity of the tether to shine when I got there, but the feeling was far less prominent than it had been in the Throne Room. It must've been all in my head. I swung open the door, and sure enough, Melany lay nude and strewn across my red satin sheets alongside an orange haired girl who shyly covered herself with her arms. I scanned the room, looking for the third tribute.

"Where is she?" I spat. "I asked for three of you."

Dread pooled in my stomach as I feared the worst, that some kind of mistake had been made and the woman from the throne room, the one with the tether, had been mistakenly drained.

A knock sounded at my door and I yanked the door open to see Ronan standing in the doorway.

"Where is she?" I asked between clenched teeth. "If you drained her—"

"The tribute is in her bedroom. She refuses to join you tonight."

"Where?"

"The east—"

Before he could finish, I barreled down the hallway to the east wing. Anger and excitement was a deadly cocktail in my blood as the weight on my chest increased with each step. I threw open the double doors and rushed to the woman in the white ballgown who was standing at the center of the room like she was expecting me. I rushed forward and cornered her, my fangs hovering less than an inch from her flesh.

"Why do you refuse to join me?"

Her bottom lip trembled, but she didn't look away. "I was taken from my home. I didn't volunteer. I was told that you don't accept hostages, now let me go."

She was right, I never took anyone underage nor anyone who didn't volunteer, but now, now that this new possibility was here, this new force, I couldn't just let her go. I stepped closer. The tether pressed in on me when I saw her hand rise to her chest. I froze. *So this is a tether. . . and she can feel it, too.*

I straightened and took several steps back. "I apologize for the misunderstanding. How about you stay the night, and tomorrow I will try to make amends."

She looked unsure but nodded slightly, so I took my leave before she could change her mind, and stationed two guards outside her door, just in case.

"Ronan," I barked as I reached my door. "Send the other tributes back to their rooms. I'm tired."

Despite my words, I didn't sleep for a second. My heartbeat never slowed.

I ran through the image of the girl who refused my bed and wondered, what terrors did she have in store for me?

TWENTY

I stood at the center of my bed-chamber; my heart still racing from my encounter with the Blood King. The tether had been much more crippling than I imagined, weighing on my chest and blurring my senses to the point where I could scarcely observe him when he was standing right in front of me. In fact, my memory of our conversation was nothing but a black empty space in my mind, save for one crucial detail that remained, churning my nerves.

He too felt the tether.

This was both a danger and undoubtedly what had saved me from his brutality. Either way, from this point on, he'd be wary of me.

Just when I thought he was about to show the

cruel, angry tyrant that made up his reputation, he softened, and there was no possible explanation except for the tether. If I were to keep my wits about me long enough to seduce him, I'd have to find some way to overcome the tether myself. He might've had a moment of softness, but that didn't excuse a lifetime of wickedness.

He was a blood drinker. The bulk of the girls I'd gotten to know in the Arrow Court had already been reduced to pale corpses. If I hadn't whispered that small incantation, Mel and Celine might have been dead as well. It had been only a small bit of suggestion magic, I couldn't have risked more, but I suspected the tether might've made the incantation more effective.

Thus far, Ezra's plan was right on track. It seemed I'd be able to bargain with the King on my terms and hopefully take away the possibility of being bitten, which would surely give me away before I could complete my task. I wondered if I'd have enough sway to save my new companions as well. Though I knew I had Finn hidden away in my shadow, he could not risk leaving his shadow form, and therefore was of little comfort in a court that felt like it was drenched in blood.

I began to undress, peeling away the white fabric that labeled me as an outcast and took in a deep breath as I explored my bedroom. It was decorated much like the rest of the Blood Court. It was overly ornate, and dripping with red velvet fabric. Candelabras and decorative vases were studded with rubies and rimmed with gold accents. It felt like a natural opposite to the Arrow Court with its organic growth and wildlife. Here, everything was handchosen, gaudy, and dripping with the impersonal, judgmental feeling that all places of warship seemed to inherently carry. How fitting then that the Blood Court made their home in a refurbished cathedral. The absence of natural light should have reminded me of my home under the ground, but the stonecarved caves that made up my life were natural. Natural, like the winding branches of the Arrow Court.

I slipped into bed. The silky fabric was smoother and softer than it looked. I closed my eyes, and the blackness behind them brought a welcome piece of home. After many lifetimes of wishing to leave the shadows of my home, I missed it, and I wondered if I should have paused to enjoy it one last time, just in case I never made it back home.

I awoke feeling refreshed and well-rested, but despair quickly set in. I got up slowly and walked to the wardrobe, pulling it open to find an array of clothing, all in the exact same, empty white color as the ball gown that was still sprawled across the floor from last night. I grabbed a pair of white stretchy pants and a flowy top and threw it on the bed. A door at the side of the room caught my eye. I'd noticed it the night before but I'd been too tired to investigate. I tiptoed over to it and cracked it open to peek through, just in case someone was on the other side.

Relief rushed through me as I took a look around the private bathroom. Every surface was made of pristine, white marble, with the notable exception of the golden faucets and accents, which were a welcomed break from the red fabric. There was a large, oval shaped tub, big enough for several people at once and a vanity that was stocked with makeup, creams, hygiene items, cotton swabs, soaps, and anything else I could have imagined, down to multiple types of toothbrushes. We used magic to accomplish most matters of hygiene in the Shadow Court, and many of the items were new to me.

I was tempted to fill the tub with blankets and pillows and make this my new home, as the environment felt more welcoming than my stuffy bedroom, but I wasn't totally committed to the idea. I washed quickly, making use of a new toothbrush but giving the makeup a pass. I slipped on my new clothes and contemplated waiting until someone came to fetch me. My patience didn't hold out. I made my way to the door and peeked through. The guards on either side straightened to attention when they saw me.

"Good morning," I said, stretching my arms over my head and patting one of the guards on the back.

"Miss," he said, suddenly. "We are to escort you to the dining room for breakfast."

"Escort away."

I'd half expected him to hold his arm out and lead me to our destination, as we did in my obviously more civilized court. Instead, he stepped in front of me to lead the way while the second guard marched closely behind me.

For as ornate as the cathedral was, it felt like once you'd seen one gaudy red room, you'd sort of seen them all. It wasn't much to look at, so I thought I'd entertain myself with a little conversation. If I'm lucky, I might be able to pry some information out of them.

"I'm Sinna. What's your name?" I said, leaning forward to the guard.

He glanced back over his shoulder, but didn't speak. I was going to attempt again with another question, but the guard behind me spoke before I did.

"I'm Callum."

I grinned. "Callum, excellent. It's nice to meet you."

The guard turned back, rolling his eyes.

"See? That wasn't so hard, was it?" I teased. He turned away.

"If you don't tell me your name, I'll be forced to make one up." He stopped short in front of tall double doors, gesturing to the guards stationed in front to open them.

He narrowed his eyes, so I stepped through, looking back at him over my shoulder. "I think I'll go with. . . Grumpy."

There were more than a few guards standing around a long, redwood table and once I got a little closer to it my heart leapt with excitement. Seated at the far side of the room were Mel and Celine. Mel's mouth dropped open and Celine's eyes widened when they met mine. I hastened over and took a seat beside them, bursting with relief . They were practically strangers and yet I felt responsible for them somehow, and a little less alone. I wanted to talk to them, to ask them a million questions about their first night or their impression of the Blood King, but the number of guards hovering around us kept us silent.

The second I took my seat, a plate with a golden cover was placed in front of me.

A guard removed the lid, exposing a plate of steaming red soup. My stomach churned. Is it blood? Mel caught my eye and she lifted her spoon, picked up a scoop of white rice from a side dish, and dipped the loaded spoon into the soup before bringing it to her lips. I leaned a little closer, breathing in the scent. It smelled spicy and a little fermented. I wasn't sure what kind of soup it was, but I doubted it was made of blood. Following Mel's lead, I got a scoop of rice, and dipped it into the bowl, letting the red soup coat the white grains.

There was a loud creak behind me, which set my nerves on edge. The sound of a man's heavy footsteps grew louder, until a man with a scruffy beard walked up next to me.

"Hello, miss. My name is Ronan."

"I'm Sinna," I said, my spoon hanging in the balance.

I snuck a glance at Mel and Celine whose faces seemed to drain of color. Why did they look worried? Did they know something about this man that I did not? Did he know something about me he shouldn't?

His next words sent a pang of fear racing through me. "I need you to come with me."

TWENTY-ONE

MADDOX

*T*he light that filtered through the parlor window looked more like light from the setting sun than the blood-red of the other stained glass windows in our court. It was slightly less comfortable than rooms that more proudly displayed my court's signature color, but that was why I had chosen it for the meeting. It was the most neutral place in the east wing. I could only sit for a short time before needing to stand up and pace a bit around the room. *So, she's my tether.* The very thing that could destroy my existence and topple my reign. Why, then, did I allow her to stay overnight, and what was I hoping to accomplish with this meeting? Was it just curiosity? A test of wills greater than any other, for me to prove my dominance? Had the tether already taken hold of me?

A knock rapped at the door, and I bounded across the room to have a seat by the window.

I took a calming breath, then said, "Come in."

The door swung open, and I felt the tether tighten against my chest. I turned toward the window and felt her presence as she crossed the room. The doors clicked shut, and I gestured to the chair on the far side of the window, hoping that the distance would ease the intensity of the tether. "Please have a seat."

She obeyed, and I ventured a peek at her only to find her already staring out the window, no doubt feeling the crippling effects of the pull as much as I was.

After several seconds of silence, I forced myself to break through. "What is your name?"

"Sinna, Your Highness."

Her presence choked me. "Do you know who I am?"

"Yes, Your Highness." Her gaze moved to me, her eyes a soft brown color that was rimmed in darkness.

"And you were brought here by force?"

"Yes, Your Highness."

I exhaled my frustration. Both at the situation and my inability to feel like myself. What did I have to be nervous about? She was nothing. Just a tether, which most likely had some kind of workaround. "I don't take hostages. You're free to go, but I wonder if there was something I could tempt you with to stay."

"Why?"

I must've stared with a blank expression, because after a moment she continued. "Why do you want me to stay here? What do you want with me?"

I wasn't sure why, but I felt like the question put me at a disadvantage. "I wanted three companions to entertain me for the next few weeks, and I've gone and drained all the rest of the tributes already. So you see, you'll have to do."

She nodded thoughtfully and I felt a twinge of relief that she bought such a weak reply. "So tell me, Sinna. What is it that you want?"

"I want you to give your word that I won't be bitten by you or anyone else."

I clenched my jaw. It wasn't unreasonable, but I didn't like being denied something I so dearly wanted to sample.

She leaned forward and the tether tugged. "I'd like not to be escorted everywhere by guards."

I ran my hand through my hair. "How will I know you won't run away?"

"You don't, but as you said, I'm not a hostage."

I clicked my tongue. "That won't do. Once you volunteer to be here, I can do with you what I want. How about you exchange your vow for mine. I'll promise you won't be bitten, and you won't be followed by my guards, and you'll promise not to leave."

She leaned back in her chair, crossing her arms over her chest. "Fine, but I have one more request."

She piqued my interest. "Oh? And what is that?"

"Immortality."

Disappointment was a silver stake through my chest. How boring. She was the same as all the others.

She turned to the window, allowing me to observe her face more closely without suffering under the weight of her gaze.

"Not for me. For the other two girls, Melany and Celine."

"You don't want immortality?"

She turned to me and lanced me with her next words. "Why would anyone want that?"

I bit my tongue to avoid hurling reasons at her. It was the ultimate prize, sought out by the world, and desired by all. Wasn't she begging me to make her little friends immortal? Immortality was mine, and mine alone to give and yet, no one had ever asked me that question before.

The tether tightened, so I stood quickly, pacing to the far side of the room in hopes of relief.

"I will not guarantee immortality to anyone. But I can offer them relative safety as long as they obey the rules of my manor."

She stood, closing the gap between us, tightening the tether with each brazen step. "Do we have a deal?"

My eyes narrowed. "Answer one more question for me, and we'll consider our business finished."

She bit on her bottom lip before her face brightened. "Excellent. I have a question of my own. Yours first, of course, Your Highness."

I eyed her. She was an obvious beauty, but many of the tributes were. It was a trait I felt nearly numb to, but unlike the others, her arms and hands were free of the scars and burns of the brutal labor that drove the mortals to my door. If not for immortality, what reason other than desperation or stupidity would tempt her to stay? Could it be the tether?

Rather than show her all of my cards, I asked simply, "Why stay?"

She held my gaze, and when she spoke, it was barely a whisper. "Curiosity."

I understood. That was the force that drove me as well.

She looked into my eyes like my thoughts were hers to read, and several moments passed in weighted silence before I found my voice. "And your question?"

"When are you going to let me leave?"

The thought of this new and interesting challenge walking out of my life left a bad taste in my mouth, but she wouldn't be new or interesting forever. I'd lose interest just as I had with the others before her.

"When the time comes."

TWENTY-TWO

I was more than eager to leave the King's presence, partly because of the tether and the grueling physical symptoms it always manifested, but also because of the King's frightening attractiveness. It was worrisome that I'd only been in the Blood Court for a single day, and I already struggled to look away. His sharp jawline, pale skin, blood-stained lips, and piercing white fangs were one thing, a jumble of features that came together in a ruthlessly seductive combination, but his eyes were what captured my interest the most.

When I first saw him, I would have said with certainty that they were black, but now that I'd seen them closer, they flared red without warning like hot coals in the wind. He seemed wary to get too close, and I couldn't blame him. The tether was brutal, painful even, but that did nothing to stop my imagination from running wild, imagining all the ways his eternity of lust could satisfy me.

But even if the tether wasn't an issue, my orders were clear. I was to avoid sleeping with the Blood King as long as possible in order to fuel his frustration. Thus far, Ezra's plan hadn't failed me. I'd been able to negotiate away my worst fear and although I couldn't save Mel and Celine absolutely, I was sure they were safe for a while at least. As I roamed through the carpeted halls, I realized I was more than a little aimless. I'd asked for more freedom and privacy, and in turn, the King had called off his guards. I wasn't very familiar with the court's layout, so I retraced my steps to the dining room with hopes that Mel and Celine would still be there. The guards opened the door, and I headed inside to find Celine polishing off the last of my soup. The room was still filled with guards, and I wished they'd clear out so I could chat freely with the girls for the first time since we had arrived. We were forced to sit beside each other, too afraid to reveal anything in the presence of the enemy. A few minutes later a bearded guard that I recognized from earlier, entered. "The King has reassigned the guards to concentrate their efforts on the perimeters of the court."

"Yes, Ronan," they said in unison, as they made their way out of the room.

Ronan approached the table, drawing our full attention. "The King is granting you all free roam of the Blood Court. You are welcome to explore, but you may not leave the cathedral unescorted. I suggest you avoid the kitchen, both to stay out of the servants' way, and also to spare yourself a potentially gruesome shock. Otherwise any forbidden areas or rooms will remain locked or heavily guarded for your protection, of course. Meals will be served three times a day in this very room. You need only to enter and ask a guard to have something made for you, and you are at the King's beck and call, no matter what time of night he requires your entertainment. I'm sure I needn't explain the consequences for violating any of these rules."

He smirked at our blank stares as if pleased with his speech, then he took his leave. We waited several minutes before any of us dared to look around and make sure we were really alone. Celine squealed with delight. "He picked us!" she said, beaming, her hand tightly gripping my wrist.

"I'm so glad you're both okay."

"Us?" Mel asked. "You refused the Blood King. We were terrified that he killed you."

I suppressed a smile. "You do care."

Her mouth straightened to a hard line. My mind was wracked with curiosity. If I couldn't touch the King myself, I could at least get some insight on whether I should be torturing myself by imagining it. "So, what happened last night? Did you guys sleep with the King?"

Mel leaned back in her chair.

"No, we were both in his bed but he got angry when you didn't come and we were asked to return to our rooms." Her orange curls bounced with every move of her head. "He's gorgeous, right? Mel won't admit it, but she was as excited to be with him as I was." She sighed, resting her head on her hand. "To think we almost slept with an immortal king."

Celine was sweet, endearing me to her with her little mortal point of view, but Mel was much more guarded. Both Mel and Celine had made full use of their makeup supply but it almost made me miss the quirks of their mortal faces.

I eyed Mel. "So is it true? You were excited to sleep with the King?"

The corners of her mouth tipped up. "I want to know what happened when you went to see him and why he pulled you away from breakfast. Are you sleeping with him?"

Her jealous tone caught me off guard and I felt the smallest tug on my shadow from Finn reminding me to stick to my plan. "No. Actually, I. . . I've never actually done that before."

I half expected them both to burst out laughing, because the lie was so severe, I was certain no one would buy it.

Celine's eyes bulged. "You're a virgin?"

I chewed on my tongue to stop from laughing. Virginity was such a mortal concept, so arbitrary and bizarre. I was glad to have Celine around to feed me the mortal perspective before I had to convincingly feed the lie to the King.

Mel smirked. "He's going to be so angry. I've heard that's a major turn off for him."

She was right. There wasn't an immortal on earth who didn't prefer someone with experience, but it might help me avoid sleeping with the King even if just for a short time.

I didn't appreciate Mel's smugness. She had her eye on the prize, seemingly rooting for Celine and I to fail so she could have a greater chance to win over the King, but that might work to my advantage. She smirked at her soup, as if basking in her sexual prowess, when I'd likely slept with more people than she'd ever come in contact with.

"Yeah," I said. "I'm hoping to keep it a secret."

"I promise not to tell," Celine said.

We both looked at Mel who nodded, but didn't make eye contact. We spent the rest of the day attempting to explore the Blood Court, but it felt like every door was locked. The hallways were clear except for an occasional stranger, who always ducked into the nearest room and locked it before we passed. We returned to the dining hall for lunch and dinner, and I found it interesting when Celine compared our day's activities to her experience as a child in summer camp. I had assumed we'd see more of the King during the day, but after I left the parlor, I didn't see him again. There were still many hallways to explore and more locked doors to test. We hadn't even stumbled across the forbidden kitchen, but we felt more at ease chatting when we knew for sure we were alone, so after dinner we returned to our rooms.

When we returned, we discovered that our bedrooms were in the same hallway and no longer had guards stationed out front. The rooms were identical, but the clothing choices varied. They all were made of the same, empty, white color but were drastically different in style. We lay them all out and traded for the styles that suited us best. Celine went for the more flowy garments, Mel chose the sexiest, while I made sure to get the least remarkable options.

We were all in my room chatting to pass the time, when someone rapped at the door.

I jumped, startled. "Come in."

Ronan opened the door. "The King has requested all of you to his bedchamber. You have five minutes to ready yourself."

TWENTY-THREE

*A*fter my negotiations with Sinna, I spent the afternoon hidden away in the library. I knew the council would be annoyed that I wasn't there to approve any new immortals. Even my least despised council member, Aiko had messaged her annoyance that I hadn't been more involved, but I had a more pressing matter at hand.

The tether.

Since it was a natural immortal occurrence, it had to have some countermeasure, as was the nature of all things. Normally I'd delegate such a time-consuming task, but if anyone found out that I had a tether to Sinna, she'd be killed on the spot. It wasn't like I was going to fall in love with her, there was no risk of that. My fascination was with testing my limits, which was more than a little unsettling to

Ronan, and whoever started the treasonous whisperings that had become rampant among our kind. The library was endless, centuries of information stored under the Blood Court's protection.

It had been many years since I'd stepped foot in that room, and based on the amount of dust that rose into the air each time I pulled a tome from the shelf, it had been a while since anyone else had either. Occasionally, I stumbled across a book which triggered nostalgia from a past read, and I'd set it aside.Over the course of the day that stack grew. Book after book, hour after hour, and there was scarcely a mention of the tether in anything. I was starting to lose hope when I came across a historical book we'd stolen from the Moon Court. It spoke of a jeweled necklace that the Moon Court's mortal queen wore until her death. I abandoned my search for mentions of the tether, focusing on the necklace, and the more I looked into it, the more convinced I grew that that necklace could suppress the tether.

I sat down at the table, exhausted but satisfied when Ronan busted in.

He eyed me suspiciously. "What are you doing, Sire?"

The books in front of me were the harmless ones I'd stumbled across, and the ones I used for research were already tucked back onto the shelves. "I was gathering some reading material."

"Bored with your tributes already?"

"Shouldn't that be a relief to you?"

He crossed his arms and took a seat at the chair across from me. "I'm not worried. You may as well have said, 'I'll take any three.'"

I smiled at his dimwitted appraisal. "And how do you find them?"

"Unremarkable. I doubt they'll survive the week. You didn't even care to station guards outside their bedrooms."

I shrugged. "It seemed like a waste of resources."

He sighed, so relieved with the tributes he assumed were failures, that he didn't badger me about skipping the council meeting.

I thumbed through the book in front of me, and Ronan eyed in only to settle quickly back into his peace.

"Ro, I was thinking of inviting Herod over for dinner. Can that be arranged?"

He straightened. "Sire, revenge will only lead to—"

"It's not for revenge. Just a gesture of peace."

His eyes narrowed. "Will your tributes be dining with you as well?"

"Of course not. Just me and the Moon King."

He stood. "Yes, Sire. I'll have him informed of your invitation."

"Have the tributes ready in my bed chamber when I'm finished."

"Yes, Sire."

He bowed and left me with my dusty stack of books. I had a few hours to come up with a plan to get into the Moon Court and snoop around. I'd be watched closely from the moment I stepped foot there, and it wasn't like I could ask around about the necklace without revealing my extremely dangerous and complicated plan with Sinna. The wolves would literally descend on my court.

I needed chaos. Herod could be nudged into action. I just needed to be cautious about which action to take.

A few hours later I had a decent plan in place. Herod arrived and I met him in the guest dining room for dinner.

"Still no shirt, I see."

"How would you know what a real man looks like if I didn't show you one every now and then? Besides, I wore my finest paint."

I smirked at him, but I could tell that a lot of the tension was genuine. We took a seat at the table.

"Relax, I wish you no harm."

"I heard you got sick after draining my tributes. I assure you I had nothing to do wi—"

"Water under the bridge. I invite you here to mend any discourse between us."

Our servants entered, carrying trays of raw, partially bloody steak. Herod couldn't hide the smile that crept onto his face. We ate, and each bite seemed to dull our tension.

He chewed happily, chatting to me between bites. "I hear you have some new favorites."

"Three new guests."

"Anyone special?"

I shrugged. "Are you jealous I kept some of Delton's tributes and not yours?"

He grinned.

I saw my opening and went for it, but it was an offer I'd never made as it slightly shifted the power dynamic, even if just for an evening. "I was thinking that it's been some time since you've held a ball at the Moon Court."

He slowly lowered his fork. "It would be my honor, if it pleases you."

"It would, and I'm certain Delton would also appreciate an invitation."

He perked up and I took it as a sign that when it

came down to it, Delton would side with Herod and not with me. It would be an interesting tidbit to share with Ronan later. Herod nodded. "You shall name the day."

"Tomorrow night."

He stared at me, but I challenged his gaze with my own. Surely it would be an excellent opportunity for him to show the wealth and stability of his court as well as network, all while on his own grounds. It might've slightly put me out, but with so much going on, it could've opened an opportunity to seek out the necklace. Of course, one night didn't give Herod much time to plan a large event, but he wasn't the type of man to back down from a challenge.

We finished our meal shortly after. I invited the Wolf King to a nightcap, but he refused, stating politely that he needed to go make preparations for the ball the next night. I was happy to wish him adieu, because I knew my tributes were waiting. Tether or not, tonight I'd test my limit and tomorrow I'd get that necklace and that limit would be no more.

TWENTY-FOUR

*T*he tether tugged as the King drew closer to his bedroom, sending my heartbeat racing. Celine had chosen a white baby doll with furry panties for tonight, while Mel went for a lacy corset complete with garters and heels. I chose a modest silk nightgown that stopped just above the knee. *Think Sin, what would a virgin do?*

I took a seat on a bench by the window while the other girls lay across the bed like treats on a tray of desserts. I felt silly and out of my element, hidden in my lie. Unlike the Hunters, creeping through the shadows to take out their targets, I had to wilt when I was born to take control. Not to mention pass up a night with the Blood King.

I wasn't used to denying myself things I wanted, or forgoing pleasure for any reason. When I'd first

156

heard my sister's plan it had sounded counterproductive. If my ultimate goal was to seduce the Blood King, why did I have to refrain from sex as long as he'd allow? But I was in the habit of trusting my sister and she had never steered me wrong before.

The King pushed through the doors, startling us all. The guards promptly closed them behind him. His gaze met mine immediately, and in one smooth motion he pulled off his shirt, revealing a chiseled body that made my mouth drop open involuntarily. He marched straight toward me, the tether throbbing in my chest as I swallowed a mouthful of lust, that manifested as a lump in my throat.

"Get in the bed," he said, his eyes flaring a deep red.

I stood, inching toward the bed while keeping my distance, anything to lessen the intensity of the pull on my chest toward him. I sat on the edge. I glanced at Celine and Mel. Celine was mesmerized by the King's bare chest, but Mel's face caught my attention. Her lips were pursed, and her eyes were rolled back in pure annoyance. I remembered our conversation earlier, it didn't seem like it would take long for Mel to spill about my supposed virginity. The King walked over and sat on the bed, the silky fabric beneath me tugging from his weight.

He reached for Celine, pulling her in for a kiss, while Mel's hands slid over the King's pants, making their way to the strings around his waist. A blush washed over me as I watched them, enamored by the sight. His hand rose, reaching out to me. I wanted to take it, to surrender to the tether and take my share in the delight to come, but I couldn't. I'd taken this mission with a promise to my sister that I would stick to her plan at all costs. I needed to prove I was still in control. I let his hand hang there, as he worked Celine's strap off her shoulder and kissed down her neck.

He pulled away, his black eyes glaring at me, rage flaring behind them. "What is your problem?"

Mel sighed loudly. "She's a *virgin*."

I stared at her wide-eyed and betrayed, though she'd filled her role perfectly.

"What?" she said. "You were making it so obvious."

The King stood, rubbing his palm across his face, his silk pajama pants bulging. When he dropped his hand, I could see that everything that Mel said was true. He really did hate virgins. I knew exactly how this was going to go. I would be banished back to my room and have to beg Celine and Mel for details tomorrow, but the King looked ready to strangle me.

When he finally spoke, it was through his teeth. "Is it true?"

I swallowed hard. "Yes, but it's not a big deal. If you just tell me what to do—"

"Not a big deal? Tell you? What can a novice possibly offer me? I'll settle for nothing less than a competent lover." He marched over to me and I winced from the tether, half expecting him to strike me. He lifted me, cradling me in his arms as he carried me across the room before dropping me onto a chair. He yanked the tie off the nearby curtain and used it to bind my arms behind me. Then he proceeded to drag the chair to the side of the bed.

He took a deep breath through his nose, and I could practically feel his frustration in his exhale. "Watch and learn."

"Why are my hands tied?"

He turned away. "Just in case."

What might've been meant as a punishment was anything but. Sure, it was a little hard to watch without hope of release, but I could take care of that when I got back to my own room.

Then he started. Fuck. *I might not be as in control as I thought.*

Once again, he started with Celine, pulling her top off over her head. She radiated with pleasure as he tasted her one lick at a time, but Mel wasn't going to give up so easily. She slid her hands under the waistband of his pants and began to work him. His head turned to her, his hands dropping from Celine and moving to Mel. He pulled off his pants and Mel's stringy thong at the same time. I strained to get a look at his equipment, but Celine was in the way. She crawled over to them, searching for something to do, but she'd already lost the King's interest. Before I could get a good look, he thrust into Mel, her pleasure ringing out through the room, as desire blared between my legs.

I felt wetness seep between my legs as he wrapped her ponytail around his wrist and drove into her. Harder and harder until she was pressed against the headboard. Celine's face was wrought with despair, but she didn't matter. Nothing mattered but the sounds ringing in my head, and the sweat that slipped down the Blood King's face as he brought Mel to ecstasy and, without pause, repeated the process. I pulled on my binding, begging myself not to give in to the temptation to join, and breathed through the flimsy tie.

That's when I felt the shadow between my legs

move. *No Finn. He'll catch us.* Finn's fingers slipped into me. I remained perfectly still as Finn synced with the King's rhythm. I imagined he had me pressed against his headboard, filling my body with waves of pleasure. I didn't make a sound and instead imagined that my voice echoed through the King's chamber. The King sped up, with Mel bucking as she came to her third orgasm.

Finn's fingers challenged my body not to grind against him. Then the King's attention snapped to me, my eyes widening as my body exploded into orgasm. His body jerked, his eyes clamping shut as he hunched over Mel. The spasms between my legs slowed, but I didn't dare move a fraction. After a few moments, the King got up and walked towards me, his penis in full view-- still pulsing as the last bits of cum dripped from the tip. My mouth dropped open as I sat balanced perfectly between the fear of being caught and the desire to participate.

His eyes narrowed as he leaned over me. "Get the fuck out," he said, then he turned to Celine. "You too."

Mel sat up straight as Celine untied me, tears already streaming down her face, as we scrambled toward the door.

"Compose yourself," we heard him say. "We're going again."

I felt my first bite of jealousy as Celine and I walked to our rooms. No matter, my shadow was going to fuck me until the sun came up.

TWENTY-FIVE

I closed my eyes and listened for footsteps outside my bedroom, but I hadn't heard anyone pass in hours. I might've been entertaining a bit of risky behavior but that didn't mean I wanted to blow the whole operation.

"What's with you tonight, Sin?" Finn whispered, through the darkness.

"Get up, we're fucking again."

"I'm serious. Talk to me. Is that guy getting to you already?"

I sat up. "What? No. He strapped me to a chair and made me watch. Of course I'm horny."

"That's why I helped you along. I've never seen you like this. I've never seen you rally this quickly or go so many times in a row."

I groaned and straddled him, as I started slowly grinding against him.

"I'm fine," I said. "I just can't get enough of you tonight."

I felt him start to harden between my thighs, so I slipped him inside me and began to ride. He slowly worked his way back into it, but I knew he was right to be concerned. It wasn't him I couldn't get enough of. I was chasing something. A feeling I couldn't find no matter how many times I came. I forced him back into shadow form before first light, as the possibility of anyone casually strolling by my room grew the longer I allowed it to continue, but I couldn't get to sleep. I took a long bath, dozing off for a few minutes before I pulled my pruney body out of the tub, and got ready for the day. I decided to head to breakfast, if for nothing else, to take a break from my own thoughts, only to find Celine already seated at the table. I took a seat beside her, and her somber mood seemed to match mine.

I'd barely thought of her all night, but I was sure she was equally frustrated by the night's events. The King seemed to go for her right away, but Mel had completely edged her out of the picture. At least I had the excuse of being tied to a chair. We sat in silence for a full hour, pushing things around on our plate, letting the mood overtake us until the doors swung open and Mel limped in.

She wasn't moving well and she winced when she sat down at the table. I pretended not to notice even though all I could do was notice every micro movement. Her eyes flared with smugness but she matched our somber mood as best as she could with the rest of her face.

"Sorry I outed you as a virgin," she said. "And Celine, I didn't see where you went. I got so caught up."

The words shot out of me before I could stop them. "How was your night?"

Her face brightened. "I know you both are upset with me, but you don't understand."

A servant entered, and we all went quiet while he placed a plate of food in front of her. *Oh I can't wait for this explanation.*

"There's this like. . . cosmic connection between us. I was wrong about him, and I think he's found what he's looking for. I just hope you two can find a way to be happy for us."

I faked a cough to muffle a laugh. Suddenly draining mortal tributes for their blood seemed pretty victimless. I didn't care that she got to spend the night with the King. That was my plan. In fact, if I was lucky, she'd spend many more nights with him before I ever saw his bedroom. I might've considered the entire situation as amusing, but Celine looked like she was going to burst into tears at any moment. Luckily someone knocked, stealing the moment, and we turned to see Ronan stride in.

"Good morning, ladies. The King has requested that you all attend a ball tonight at the Moon Court."

I gasped. The Moon Court? I was seriously going to go three for three on this mission?

I snuck a glance at Mel and Celine who both looked a little confused, so I mirrored their expression but Ronan didn't pause to elaborate.

"You will be measured and styled, commencing after you finish eating. It should go without saying, but you are expected to only speak highly of the King and anything regarding the Blood Court."

"You don't have to worry about that," Mel said, flashing a smile.

"Indeed," he said warily. "I too will be in attendance and will be keeping an eye on all of you. If anyone crosses the line of what I consider acceptable behavior, the consequences will be dire. Do you understand?"

I nodded but inside I was practically screaming with excitement. I was the greatest Hunter on earth. In a matter of days, I'd infiltrated all of the immortal courts. Oh, if Ferah could see me now.

All day I imagined what the Moon Court might be like, barely present as the servants spent the day preparing me for the party. My body was stuffed into a white, floor-length ball gown and I was given gloves that went nearly up to my shoulders, along with a fur wrap, but my mind was already in the Moon Court.

I paced around my room, waiting for someone to come collect me, when Finn slithered out of shadow form.

"What are you doing?" I whispered. "Get back. They'll be here any minute."

"I can't go with you."

"What? Why?"

"There's a small possibility one of the wolves could smell me. We can't risk it. I'm going to stay here and shadow your bed until you get back."

"But—"

"We don't have time to discuss this. Just stay out

of trouble at the ball and get back safely, no matter what."

Before I could respond, I felt his weight lift from me and saw a flash of darkness slip under my bed. My excitement drained as fear filled its place. I was alone, and somehow for the first time since I'd arrived, the danger felt real.

TWENTY-SIX

*T*he sun was already peeking over the tree line and through the stained glass window as Melany snored loudly on the far side of my bed. All night I had chased the satisfaction of that first release, but none had come close. I could only assume that looking at Sinna had pushed me over. But how could it? I certainly wasn't interested in wasting my time with a virgin. But all night I pictured her blushing face as I asked her to leave. All night, I'd replaced Melany in my mind with Sinna, chasing that feeling to no avail. To Melany's credit, she knew what she was doing, and for a mortal, her endurance had held out longer than I'd anticipated. It was clear by morning that she couldn't satisfy me, not anymore.

The day moved at a glacial pace as I visualized

every possible scenario at the ball, none of which ended with me finding the necklace. It was a small object and there was no guarantee it even still existed. Even worse, the entire Moon Court would be swarming with wolves and I doubted they let anyone have free roam of their court, especially not their natural enemy--but after last night, I was desperate to dull the effects of the tether without killing Sinna. For the time being, she still intrigued me and that warranted a little more time. Then I saw her standing in the hallway, dressed in white. Her hair was pinned back out of her face so she couldn't hide behind it as she so often did. The tether tugged on my chest and took me several moments to realize she was standing with the other two girls. The tether choked my air supply, and I forced the struggle away from my expression as I walked to the ladies, offering Celine and Melany each an arm.

They took them eagerly, and I turned before I could see Sinna's reaction. I felt her follow behind as we walked out into the frigid winter night. We traipsed a short distance to the forest edge where an elegant dog sled sat, with two massive wolves harnessed to the front. We climbed in, and the girls huddled against my arms while Sinna took a seat across from us. Face to face, she was in my direct line of sight, and I didn't dare look away. Her gaze bore into me, but I held it.

The dog sleds were limited, usually only offered to me and Delton. They kept the trail to the woods, which stretched almost thirty minutes from my court to theirs and forty five from Delton's. I was sure Herod's pack had better things to do than chauffeur us around; still, I always appreciated the gesture. I figured that Herod insisted on keeping the tradition alive because one of the privileges of holding a ball was to show off the unique abilities and uses that our courts possessed, with the hopes of conjuring envy from our honored guests.

The dog sled bobbed between the moonlit trees, gliding across the glittering snow. The strength of the wolves was evident in each powerful stride. It was not a smooth ride, jerking with the movement of the wolves as they waded through the snow. Sinna said nothing, but her eyes were lit with excitement, as a smile played at the corners of her mouth so incessantly that I wondered if the ride was more exciting moving backward. I got my enjoyment from watching her, vibrant in the moonlight as the cold brought a pink tint to her cheeks and nose. Melany nuzzled into my arm, drawing my attention. I needed to be more careful with the slight preference

I'd developed for Sinna, at least until I got the tether situation sorted out. The wolves grew winded, clouds of breath rising above their thick coats until finally, they halted outside the Moon Court.

The stone structure that made up the court hadn't changed much since I'd last seen it, but it always looked much grander in the moonlight. The wolves shifted back to their human forms and helped us out of the sled, and I wasn't sure whether the shift or the court itself intrigued Sinna more. On the outside, her expression stayed almost neutral, but the way her eyes glittered betrayed her.

The architecture of the Moon Court was a bit unusual, an eyesore during the daytime, but at night, a series of mirrors reflected the moonlight into every inch of the space, shifting to follow it as it moved through the sky. We stepped onto a midnight blue carpet and made our way up the path. I held tight to Melany and Celine, but slowed so Sinna could walk beside us. The doors opened, and two snow-white wolves flanked King Herod as he welcomed us with open arms. He wore his typical paint but had a fur cape draped over his shoulders, and a silver crown on his head.

I suppressed a groan.

One ball and he thinks he's King of the world.

The nerve. I snuck a glance at Sinna and her chest was puffed out as if she was holding her breath. A pang of jealousy threatened to run through me, but I quickly got the better of it, as I remembered the reason I'd gone through the trouble.

Herod grinned. "Welcome, Your Majesty. These must be your new favorites."

I tried to match the kindness in his tone, but I hardly sounded genuine. "This is Melany, Celine, and that's Sinna."

His eyes lingered on Sinna for a few seconds too long before he caught himself. "Well, come in and enjoy the party. King Delton arrived not five minutes before you."

Herod looked down at one of his wolves, and the creature twisted into a man in a matter of seconds. He walked over and took Sinna's arm and began to lead her into the party. Sinna tossed me a look over her shoulder as if to ask permission to enter, but I couldn't muster a smile.

TWENTY-SEVEN

*A*ll the frustration and fear I'd felt all day melted away the moment I stepped into the ballroom. At the center of the high ceilings was a crystal chandelier that seemed to amplify the moon light and scatter it across the room like snow, or fallen stars. The room was filled with attendees chatting with drinks in their hands, and swaying to music which was played by an orchestra tucked away in a dark corner.

The members of the Moon Court were mostly shirtless, their skin decorated with elegant blue paint. The Arrow Court members all wore shades of green, their signature white hair and pointed ears proudly displayed with ornaments and hanging jewelry. The Blood Court members all wore suits

174

and gowns in their specific shade of crimson. I was in awe of how easily everyone interacted. I wasn't sure if it was because of the occasion, or if the Moon Court just had a more relaxed environment compared to the uptight Blood Court and the elitist Arrow Court. Now that I'd seen all of the immortal courts, I firmly put the Moon Court as my top choice.

My escort bowed once we reached the center of the room and disappeared into the crowd. It was a shame as I'd gotten more attention from that silent stranger than the Blood King since I arrived in his court. Whatever the plan had been, I needed to start deviating, and gaining his favor. He didn't seem remotely interested, and if I didn't do something, Mel would have me tossed out before I could fulfill my purpose. I was surprised to see a familiar face among the crowd, the intense green eyes met mine from across the way and I froze in place as King Delton made his way to me. He handed me a flute of sparkling wine.

"Hello again."

I bowed. "Your Highness. I hope you're well."

"Quite well, thank you. Where has your Sire run off to tonight?"

I shrugged. "I'm sure he's around here some-where." It was a vague answer considering I knew exactly where he was at all times. The tether made sure of that.

"How do you find the Moon Court?"

I took a sip of the wine, feeling more than a little out of my element. "Enchanting."

"Do you prefer it to the Arrow Court?"

The egos of immortal kings never ceased to amaze. Of course, I preferred the Moon Court. "That's impossible, Your Majesty."

His pleased smile almost made me laugh, and I hoped I'd have the opportunity to converse a little with the Moon King as well. I'd been struck silent by his blue eyes, dark skin, and bulging muscles. I never thought I'd enjoy this part of my mission so much. I would have saved dancing with immortal kings to the type of girl I was pretending to be, but at present I was taking immense pleasure in the night's festivities.

Mel draped her arm over my shoulder. "There you are, Sinna," she said with a forced smile. Her gaze moved to my glass. "And uhm, where did you get a drink?"

Celine joined us a moment later, looking dejected.

"Allow me," King Delton offered before he hurried away in search of a servant with a drink tray.

"You look beautiful tonight, Celine. "

The comment made her stand a little straighter. "Thanks, Sinna. This place is magical."

Mel scoured the crowd. "I wonder where Maddox snuck away to."

She wasn't going to find him here as he was in the next room, walking very slowly from the feel of it. I wasn't sure how long I'd have before Mel found him and clung to him for the rest of the night, so I had to find a chance to slip away. All I needed was a minute with the Blood King to try to get back on his good side. When King Delton returned, Mel took the glass from him and resumed her search without so much as a second glance.

"Mel, Celine, have you met King Delton of the Arrow Court?"

Mel whirled back to the group. "*King* Delton? Your Majesty. I had no idea we had the honor."

"I knew." Celine chimed in. "I saw you once when I arrived at the Arrow Court."

I slipped away as the two girls found a new King to fawn over, and when I was out of sight, I headed out of the ballroom towards the pull of the tether. I ducked into the hallway and into the next room. The walls were covered with bookshelves with the occasional space for a gold-trimmed family portrait. The midnight blue curtains were open, allowing the moonlight to spill across the floor. On the far side of the room, the Blood King stared into a glass box, his arms crossed over his chest, his focus completely locked in on whatever was inside that case.

The music from the orchestra wafted through the open door, but I expected him to look up when he heard my footsteps approaching. He didn't and then I remembered that, like me, he probably knew exactly where I was at all times. As I neared, I looked into the glass case where a headless bust displayed a diamond necklace.

"Alone at last," he said, without looking away.

A pang of anxiety shot through me. Did he mean because Finn wasn't here? Did he know who I was? The calmness in his demeanor assured me that he only meant that Celine and Mel weren't with me as they always seemed to be.

"Your Highness, I want to apologize. I feel like we've gotten off to an interesting start."

He kept his gaze on the necklace. "Interesting, indeed."

"May I ask why you're out here by yourself."

His gaze moved to me, and the tether tightened in my chest.

"May I ask how you found me?" He smirked and I saw a devious glint in his eyes as he watched me wrestle with whether or not to answer.

"What's with the necklace?"

"I don't know." He closed the gap between us. "I suppose I like it." The tether strained against me, and I swallowed a lump in my throat as I held my ground.

He stared down at me, his charcoal gaze sweeping over my face. "When I like something, I have to have it."

"So, take it," I whispered.

His eyes flared red and cooled back to black as he smiled down at me. Then he turned back to the case. "Alas, it's protected by something."

He reached for the case and the moonlight flared in front of his hand, like light bouncing off an iron shield.

He crossed his hands behind his back and strolled past me. "We better get back to the party before we're missed."

He didn't wait for me to follow and instead left

me with my thoughts as I felt the tether ease one step at a time. His aloofness was grating on me, especially after I'd seen him be affectionate with Mel all night. The way he crossed his hands behind his back like that, it was like the thought of touching me repulsed him. I thought if I apologized, spoke to him one on one, he'd warm up a little, but if anything, he seemed less interested than when I had first arrived at the Blood Court.

I turned back to the case with the necklace, tracing my fingers over the glass. The moonlight shone off the case and the shield protecting it showed itself once more. Interesting. A shield of light. Certainly, taking the necklace would be a risk, but it might be my only chance to turn the head of the Blood King.

The shield felt strong. It would have drawn a lot of attention if the King had tried to smash through. But the thing about light was, the stronger it was, so too was the shadow.

Before I lost my nerve, I focused my attention on the shadow. It deepened the closer I reached to the shield. I let my fingertips slip into the shadow, moving through both the shield and glass. I heard something move outside the door so I yanked the necklace into the shadow and pulled it back through the glass searching for a place to stash it.

"There you are," a voice said from behind me.

I turned to see Ronan standing in the doorway. "It's not polite to snoop. I must insist you return to the ballroom immediately."

I squeezed the necklace so tightly in my hand that I felt it dig into my skin, I took several steps toward Ronan, with the hopes he wouldn't see the empty display case and get suspicious. "Sorry, I just love libraries."

His blank expression gave me the impression he wasn't amused. I rushed by him, but he caught my wrist squeezing so tightly a yelp escaped my lips. I opened my hand and the necklace slipped out into his hand.

"What's this?"

Straining from the pain of his grip, I said, "It fell off, I was going to ask Celine to help me put it back on."

"Allow me," he said, dropping my wrist.

I rubbed at the lingering pain, and contemplated cursing him as he clasped the necklace at the back of my neck. I nearly gasped as a weight lifted off my chest. The tether was completely stripped away in an instant.

"All better, now back to the party."

Before I could move the Blood King bounded around the corner, his eyes wide, his dark hair disheveled.

"What happened?" he said, his chest heaving.

Ronan's brow furrowed. "I found this one wandering around alone, but she'll be joining the party immediately."

The King's gaze moved to my wrist, alerting me that I was still rubbing it. I dropped my hands to my side.

He glared at me. "This is unacceptable behavior. Ronan, join the others in the ballroom, I'll handle this."

Ronan smiled, as he slipped out of the room, shutting the door behind him. I turned frightened by the King's sudden intensity.

"Where were you?" he said, his voice much harsher than before. I stumbled back until my back pressed against the bookshelf.

"I was—"

His gaze moved to the necklace and all at once the color seemed to return to his face. "How did you get that?" His tone was filled with relief.

"You said you wanted it."

His head dropped, tension draining from his shoulders.

His next words came out as a whisper. "I thought I lost you."

He could have only meant the tether, but I wasn't sure what caused it to stop. He was inches away from me and I could barely feel it. "I-I'm sorry."

His gaze met mine and he moved closer, resting his forehead on mine, as his breaths slowed. My heart slammed into my chest. What was this? Or rather, who was this? His hand closed around mine and he lifted it up to the side of his cheek.

"Did he hurt you?"

"I-I'm fine."

He sighed. "I'll talk to him." He released my hand and reached around to the back of my neck. "I have to take this. I wouldn't want you to get in trouble."

His lips were so close I could feel the warmth of his breath on them. He paused, his gaze lowering to my lips. He ran his thumb over the bottom lip, but shook the thought away.

"Please," I whispered, the word escaping against my will.

He smiled, reached around, unhooked the clasp and stepped away with the necklace. The tether slammed into my chest, knocking the wind out of me. I put my palm on my stomach to settle myself as the Blood King made his way to the door.

"That's why you wanted it."

He smirked at me over his shoulder then held a finger to his plump lips, before returning to the rest of the party.

TWENTY-EIGHT

I'd been on edge since Maddox first invited me to dinner. I knew he was still furious that an underage tribute snuck into my last batch, but when rumors circulated that the Blood King got sick after he'd drank the blood of my offerings, I was prepared for the worst. I'd expected a duel, or at the very least a cruel act of revenge, but as I sat down to dine with him, he was more at ease than I'd seen him in a hundred years.

The only wrench he threw at me was the insistence that I hold a ball on short notice which at the end of the day was more of an opportunity than a punishment. I couldn't help but wonder if Delton's supposed match had somewhat tempered his cruelty. I'd heard the King had chosen three tributes to keep him company, and I hoped he'd bring them to our dinner, but I wasn't so lucky.

The night of the ball, Maddox arrived with his three trophies at his side but I knew in an instant which he favored. Two of the women were draped on his arms, and the third, he could hardly look at her. Arranging the event hadn't been much of a challenge, when I informed my pack of the Blood King's request they were eager to show our improved numbers and wealth to the other courts.

Everything got started without a hitch, with the members of each court mingling and enjoying the ambiance we'd worked to perfect, until an hour into the festivities when a foul smell set my entire back on edge. It was only there for a moment, but my people knew the salty unmistakable scent of a Shadow Mage's spell, ever since the last war. There was only one possible explanation.

The Shadow Mage Delton used to find the Blood King's mate was somewhere in the Moon Court.

I scanned the crowd for Delton, anger bringing my blood to a boil. *How dare he bring that witch here?*

I heard his boisterous laughter before I spotted him chatting with some bloodsuckers by the orchestra, a surefire way to tell he was already drunk. He met my gaze before I made it to him, his smile dying in an instant. He excused himself politely and met me a few strides away from his group.

"What is it, Herod? You look perturbed."

"How dare you bring that disgusting rodent here."

His brow furrowed and he looked around the room, before shaking his head. "I don't know what you mean."

My canines sharpened, jutting past my bottom lip. "The witch," I hissed under my breath.

He looked around nervously, taking me by the arm and leading out of earshot of the other guests. "I told you that in the strictest confidence. It is not safe to discuss such things here. It seems you are mistaken. That which you fear is under guard in the Arrow Court and I'll thank you not to mention it again."

His green eyes had a hint of anger behind them, but were otherwise full of absolute certainty. The scent still lingered in the ballroom, and several pack members exchanged glances with me, but it was Tren that approached me.

I bowed my head to Delton. "I apologize," I said with a laugh, patting him on his shoulder. "I suppose I've had too much to drink."

Delton glared at me, so I nicked a champagne

flute from a passing tray and handed it to him. He sipped it and turned back to join the party.

Tren waited until Delton was long gone before he approached.

"We've tracked the smell to the study," he said, already leading the way. I'd maintain my human form as long as possible but I couldn't help the horrors of the war from slipping into my head. What awaited me in the study wasn't what I expected, though equally dangerous.

I stopped short. Ronan stood staring into the display case for one of the Moon Court heirlooms. The smell was weaker but the study was definitely its place of origin, right around where Ronan was standing. However, I knew for sure Ronan wasn't a Shadow Mage. He was one of the most famous Vampires to fight in the war.

He smiled when he saw me, seemingly unaware of whatever had transpired in this room a few minutes before, but then again, he was a born liar.

"I didn't mean to snoop, I just needed a break from the crowd. What a lovely collection of books you have here."

I walked over to him, smelling for salt, but he smelled just like all the other bloodsuckers. Like iron. He didn't seem to mind my obvious appraisal, and instead turned back to the display case. "I must ask, though, if this case is meant to be empty."

I exchanged a loaded look with Tren, but before I could sound an alarm, I heard the shuffle of a new presence in the room.

Gigi hobbled into the room, her frail frame supported by a bejeweled walker. She was a curious case in any immortal court as immortals never aged after they reached full maturity. But Gigi had chosen a different path. She'd decided to give up her immortal life to be with her mate, and she'd lost her immortality and aged just like an ordinary mortal. Around her ninetieth birthday, she was struck with a disease that made her forget much of her life, including her mate that had been long since dead. Once the last of the memories of him faded away, her immortality resumed and she was locked in an elderly body for eternity. Though she was practically useless, too frail to shift or hunt, and too forgetful to be of use politically, she was beloved in our court for her innocence and sincerity.

"Gigi," I said quickly. "What are you doing out of bed?"

"There's a party," she said, flashing a toothless smile.

Ronan cleared his throat.

I nodded to Tren to have him escort her. "Why don't you head to it then, while I sort out a few things in here?"

"I hope this isn't about that heirloom," she said quickly.

"What do you know about that?"

She smiled coyly, delaying her response to relish in our attention. "I had it cleaned but didn't get it back into its place before the party." She took Ronan by the hand, as if they were old friends, and he slouched to meet her height. She patted him on the cheek. "We were in quite a rush you know."

This reply seemed to ease Ronan's concerns and he straightened, shaking loose Gigi's grip on his arm. "I'd better return as well, before someone notices my absence." He hurried out of the room, and Gigi's playful demeanor instantly darkened.

She waved me over like she intended to whisper, so I leaned in. She grabbed my ear and a whine slipped through my nose, prompting a laugh from Tren.

"You make a foolish king," she said bitterly. "Tren, close the door."

"What's going on, Gi?"

"Our court has the unique ability to smell shadow magic. We don't give into impulses and squander information that precious to our enemies. The heirloom was stolen using shadow magic."

I wiggled out of her grip but could not break my attention free. I rubbed my ear, my pride wounded, but unable to guess what she'd say next.

"We know that Delton has found Maddox's mate. Few know the true purpose of the heirloom, as it's been a secret kept by the Moon Court since it came into our possession, but it sheds some light on what occurred here."

"What does it do?" asked Tren.

"It dims a tether."

"You think Maddox stole it to keep himself from falling in love with his mate?" I asked her.

"I think his mate is of the Shadow Court and if there are two Shadow Mages after all this time, there may be many more."

"What are you suggesting?"

She chewed on her bottom lip before answering. "We keep everything that occurred here tonight between the three of us."

"But the last thing we want is for Maddox to dim the tether."

"It's a dangerous game to play, one he'll eventually lose. If the Shadow Court is manipulating Delton to get to Maddox, all we have to do is wait for things to play out and when the girl's plan comes to pass, and Maddox is vulnerable enough to die, we'll be ready to swoop in and finish him off while Delton deals with the consequences of letting a traitor into his court. A shift in power is coming. I suggest you put on a smile and escort me to the party."

My head spun with everything I'd learned.

How did Gigi with her scrambled memory, put together so much while I ran around impulsively accusing Delton? Gigi returned to her cheerful self, especially once we made it into the crowded ball-room. My gaze landed heavily on the woman in white at the center of the dance floor. After all this time, a Shadow Mage was Maddox's mate as well. She was as rare as she was beautiful, and I struggled to pull my attention away.

Gigi tugged on my arm and I bent down to hear her.

She whispered, "Why don't you ask that lovely girl there to dance?"

TWENTY-NINE

*S*inna was special, there was no doubt about that. I wished I had stuck around to see how she managed to free the necklace from the display case with that shield in place, but like so much about her, that was a mystery that would have to remain unsolved.

I was cheerful that because of her, I'd easily completed my objective, and could spend the night enjoying the festivities. After that encounter with Ronan, the last thing I needed was him getting suspicious about the amount of time I spent with Sinna. He was just ruthless enough to take matters into his own hands if he thought my life was on the line. I had no choice but to shower Celine and Melany with my attention throughout the party, but I wasn't expecting the consequences to affect me so severely.

With the tether still in place, I could feel Sinna's every move. It was impossible to ignore when Herod stepped in to escort her. I was sure, from what I knew of him and his eagerness to get back in my good graces, that it wasn't intentional. He probably chose to entertain her as she was left on her own for the entirety of the ball, but I still didn't like it.

Not when they danced, not when she smiled or laughed in his arms.

Melany grew bolder as the night went on, which I accredited to her alcohol consumption. Her attempts at kissing my neck or whispering in my ear made my annoyance flare, which drew pleased smirks from members of both the Arrow and Moon Courts. Eventually, I took her to a dark corner and asked her not to approach me for the rest of the night while I shifted my attention to the more reserved Celine.

With Melany pouting in the corner and Herod charming Sinna, I couldn't wait to get out of there. I stayed until a large portion of the guests had begun to head home. I said my goodbyes, thanked Herod for the ball and gathered my tributes to go.

"Stay a little longer," he insisted.

"Next time."

He seemed pleased with himself, and I had to admit, the occasion had gone without a hitch. Even Delton seemed reluctant to leave the ever-flowing trays of champagne. I wondered if I'd unintentionally altered the culture of our community by bringing back joint celebrations. I would no doubt receive a similar invitation to the Arrow Court in less than a month.

As Herod's wolves pulled the sleigh away from the Moon Court, back through the forest the way we came, Sinna shivered. I wanted to sit beside her and pull her into my arms to keep her warm, but I didn't. Instead, I wondered what passed through her thoughts as her dreamlike expression moved to the starry night sky. Melany was asleep when we arrived back at the Blood Court, so I had Ronan carry her to my chamber for the night. I figured having her there would both cause Ronan to assume I was in there and start to make him nervous enough to insist I spend time with one of the other tributes, but he was a little too drunk from the party to want to lecture me. Sinna and Celine went straight to bed, and I waited in my room until I was sure that Ronan had gone to bed. Then I headed to the drawing-room to start my preparations.

I clutched the necklace Sinna had stolen in my hand, too afraid to set it down.

It promised everything.

I was eager to see her and put it to use; to finally feel like myself in her presence. How much of the tether would remain intact? How far could I push things before I was in any real danger? They were questions I didn't know the answers to. After centuries of the same old conversations, scheming, and patterns, there was finally something new. Someone new.

I paused, my closed hand hovering an inch outside of Sinna's door.

Before I could gather myself, the door swung open and Sinna stepped into the frame. "Having trouble sleeping?"

"I'll sleep when I'm dead."

"Shouldn't be long now. At least two-thirds of the people at that party wanted you dead."

"That's quite an optimistic estimate. I was thinking of going for a walk. Would you like to accompany me?"

Her eyes brightened. "I should probably change into something."

I looked down at her sheer nightgown and quickly turned my face away before the tether strangled me to death. "Nonsense, we're not going to leave the grounds. Just put on your shoes.

She hustled into her room to retrieve them and came back quickly. I suppressed the urge to offer her my arm and crossed my arms behind my back as she fell into stride behind me. I unlocked the southern corridor and then locked it behind us, just to be sure we were alone.

She gasped. The glass windows and doors on the right side of the hallway offered a moonlit view of the atrium, complete with fully bloomed, snow-white roses which were covered in snow and doused in moonlight. She pressed her hands against the window and looked out at the motionless garden as soft white flakes began to fall. She turned to me, pleading with her eyes to go out like a puppy due for a walk.

I rolled my eyes and began pulling off my jacket before I draped it around her shoulders.

She grinned up at me.

"Don't get excited. I'm just curious about what you'd look like in red."

She bundled herself in the jacket and then said, "I've been meaning to ask you about that. You all know there are other colors, right? Yellow, orange, purple. Why are all the courts so dedicated to one color?"

I pushed open the door, and we stepped out into the frosty night air, prompting me to slip my hands into my pockets. "Tradition, I suppose. Besides, have you ever tried to wash blood out of something? It's just easier to wear red."

She flashed a smirk over her shoulder before she began to investigate the roses. "Then why are these white? Why not red roses. . . and how are they still alive in winter?"

I walked over to one and picked it. Sinna's lips parted as the white petals turned a deep crimson. When the change was complete, I handed her the flower and said, "They're blood thorns. They bloom in late fall and then freeze that way, only to die in early spring. They're as old and as rare as the members of my court."

She rubbed her shoulder with her free hand, and I couldn't move to warm her, not with the tether still in place.

"How about we get out of the cold." She nodded, and we left the way we came. She looked back at the flowers for a moment with sadness in her eyes, then clutched the rose I'd given her to her chest.

I led her to the drawing-room, where earlier in

the night, I'd stocked a fire and laid out pillows across a furry rug. I felt a pang of uneasiness about giving her the necklace because once the tether wasn't stopping me from touching her, I wasn't sure I'd be able to stop.

THIRTY

*I*t wasn't easy convincing Finn not to return to my shadow after the ball, but after I explained my close encounter with Ronan and urged him to keep an eye on him instead, he reluctantly agreed--and I was glad for it. Because at the ball, the King showed me a side of him I hadn't seen before, and I was eager to see more. My task was challenging enough without having to worry about Finn constantly asking if I'd been compromised.

I had, thus far, followed the plan to a tee, with the small exception of stealing the necklace. Based on the King's strange reaction, I'd say it was worth the gamble. Even more unusual than the King's behavior was the necklace itself. The moment Ronan put it on me, I felt the tether weaken, almost to nothing, and not a minute later did the King rush in. I'd hoped he'd let me keep it so that, at the very least, I could compose myself enough to win him over. After the King took the necklace back, I noticed a subtle change in the tether itself that I purposely didn't mention to Finn.

The tether was like gravity, pulling the King and me together. The more I fought against the sensation, the more crippling it felt, scaling up with close proximity. However if I allowed my intrigue or attraction to the King to flow freely, the tether almost felt bearable. Even as he had me pinned against a bookshelf.

When the King ordered Ronan to bring Mel to his bedchamber, I was sure I'd seen the last of him for a while, but an hour later, he arrived outside my bedroom. My mother used to tell me stories about the Blood Thorns, but I couldn't have believed their beauty until the King showed me. He had picked one and handed it to me, and I had watched with amazement as the magic took hold. On our way back inside, as I had turned to take one last look at the fabled flowers, I mistakenly pricked my thumb on a thorn. The King turned away, and I checked my thumb for blood.

My heart raced as Finn's fears echoed through

my head. Immortals couldn't bleed, not unless their immortality was compromised. As expected, there wasn't a drop on my finger, and I felt myself relax as the King led me into another locked room.

When the door opened, I walked into a wall of heat, the fireplace ablaze. My fingers were numb, and I looked at the King whose mouth curved up, granting permission. I rushed over and took a seat on the rug next to the fire, rubbing my hands in front of the flickering heat. The King took a seat beside me and stared into the flames.

"Come here," he said a few minutes later, the necklace dangling between his hands.

The tether didn't bother me as much, but I could tell by how far he chose to sit that it was still a struggle for him. I crawled over, turning my back to him and lifting my hair. His hands swept over my neck, sending a chill through my body and leaving my nipples erect.

"I want you to give this back to me at the end of tonight."

"May I ask why?"

He tilted his head to the side. *Ah. So you know where I am.* "Your Highness-" I started.

"Maddox, please."

His use of please struck me, but I didn't question

it. Everything about tonight felt informal. "Maddox." I closed my eyes, the deliciousness of his name in my mouth catching me off guard. "You seem different tonight."

He adjusted some pillows and lay across them, staring into the fire. "I'm expected to be a lot of things," he sighed. "We all are really. Sometimes I get so tired of the mundane tasks that make up each day that I can't stand the thought of tomorrow."

I shifted. "I wasn't expecting an honest answer."

"How about you give me one as well?"

My heartbeat raced. Well, whatever he wanted to know, I couldn't tell him. I'm sure no truth of mine would go over well.

I'm a spy. I'm here to kill you. I've snuck another member of my court in here.

His next words surprised me,."Tell me something true. Anything but a lie."

I thought for a moment and was sure the truest thing about me could do no harm. "I have a sister." My smile was involuntary, and his face brightened in response. I tucked a strand of hair behind my ear. "She's my favorite person."

"And your parents?"

"They died, but they were pretty great, too. I

suppose your parents are still alive, since your people are immortal."

"Actually, they died. Having children is a mortal privilege. One only reserved for someone foolish enough to fall in love."

I bent my knees and pulled them to my chest. *Well, this is awkward. I need you to fall in love with me so I can kill you.*

"I've lived a pretty sheltered life," I said, finally. "I think if I was immortal, I'd use that time to see the whole world."

"So immortality does interest you?"

I lay back, propping a pillow under my head. "I mean, you're doing such a great job selling it."

He laughed, a musical sound that I didn't know he was capable of. "I suppose not. I traveled a lot many years ago."

"And? Where's the greatest place in the world?"

"Here."

I wasn't sure if he meant his court or if there was another meaning locked away there, but I didn't have the nerve to ask. I was fairly certain he'd taken me here and gone through the trouble of getting the necklace so he could have sex with me, but he never moved closer. Instead he used the release of the tether to talk general nonsense.

The hours blurred together.

"Where would you go, Sinna, if you could travel?"

"Just Sin, please."

"Sin? As in, innocent? I'm not sure that fits."

I laughed. "Hey, I get in trouble all the time. I used to—" I stopped myself. *I used to what Sinna? Curse the servants?*

I scrambled to fill the silence with a lie, but when I looked back at Maddox, he didn't seem interested in whatever came next. He nodded, his smile dimming as if he preferred to fill in the rest himself.

Finally he sighed. "I should let you go," he said sitting up, "before anyone notices we're gone."

The bitter taste of disappointment filled my mouth. I nodded and we both stood, the last of the embers glowing beside us. I held my breath as he reached around and unhooked the necklace.

Before he walked me back to my door, before he left, he leaned in. "Speak of this to no one, and I shall come again tomorrow."

The tether tugged as I internally scolded myself for the blush that slipped onto my cheeks and the way his dark eyes made my legs jelly. It might take more than I thought to seduce Maddox, but it seemed as if I'd have another chance tomorrow. I sunk into my bed. With the morning light seeping through the tinted windows, I knew in all of my immortal days where the time seemed to drag on, none would compare to how anxiously I'd wait for tomorrow night to come.

Perhaps I'd be a Hunter yet.

THIRTY-ONE
— M A D D O X —

For the next thirty days, when I was sure Ronan was asleep, I showed up to Sinna's room and took her somewhere we could be alone. It was a hassle to invite Melany to my room several times a week, but it kept Ronan's suspicions on the wrong girl. Meanwhile, Sin and I were free to sneak away until the sun broke the horizon.

I brought the necklace to all of our secret meetings, but for some reason, I was afraid to touch her. What would happen when we crossed that line? Would the necklace be able to dull the tether enough? Would we feel differently after? Instead, we talked about everything we were able to. There were notable gaps in the stories she shared as there were with mine, things too precious to disclose to a stranger, but those secrets got more difficult to lock away. One of our favorite topics to discuss was why vampires like blood.

One night while we were strolling through the gallery, Sinna asked, "It can't taste very good. Why do you even like it?"

It took some time to compose a thought. "You know how the mortals say dying makes your whole life flash before your eyes?"

She nodded.

"Well, it's almost like we can taste it. Every feeling, every truth, every memory. Not just at the end but with every drop. It's a reminder of why we should keep living."

I was satisfied with my answer, but it only prompted more questions.

"It doesn't really sound like you want to live."

I shrugged. "If I were to die, this court would fall to infighting and probably an attack from one of the other courts. All immortal courts work this way. The safest way to pass on the throne is to appoint someone, but immortal kings and queens rarely do this. Sometimes if they find their mate, they choose to die and be together. In that case, with their immortality corrupted, they can produce an heir, but both the monarchs and their heir are extremely vulnerable to attack during this time. They rarely survive the transition."

"You did," Sinna said, looking up at me.

"Yes, but that choice started the war. My parents didn't survive, and I grew to maturity and into the full strength of my immortality without them. I was lucky that Ronan chose to protect me, instead of taking the throne for himself."

"He probably didn't want to live forever with a target on his back."

I smiled. "That's a good point."

She turned away, the way she always did when she asked a difficult question. "What do you plan on doing?"

I usually leaned toward silence before I'd resort to lying to her, but I thought she'd appreciate this particular lie. "I plan on living forever as King."

Some nights we'd go to the library, and I read some of my favorite passages to her. Her questions always surprised and entertained me. She had a strange mind. We often spoke of immortality, the sorrows of it, and I was curious about how knowingly she spoke on the topic.

We shared the unique opinion that immortality

was as much a burden as a gift, and she suggested that was perhaps the reason I was hesitant when turning new subjects to join the Blood Court.

The council had been remarkably quiet the last few weeks as if they were standing in the wings waiting for my immortality to give way so they could bleed me dry, but I was used to their treachery. I was used to them underestimating my will.

One night I instructed Ronan to send Melany to my chamber, and his face grew deadly serious. "Sire. . . the council sees you giving Miss Melany preferential treatment. They're starting to talk. I must insist you choose another tribute to accompany you for the time being. At least for a while."

I paused, as if thinking hard on the matter when I was practically bursting at the seams that this moment had finally come. "I will not be bullied, Ronan."

"Sire, I too am beginning to question whether. . . I just want to protect you. That's my job."

I put my hand on his shoulder and let out a slow breath. "Fine, send one of the other ones. Maybe Sinna."

He bowed, his demeanor immediately more cheerful. "Yes, Sire."

I closed my door and sat in my bedroom, waiting

for the door to open. I wasn't sure if it was because we were meeting in my bedroom, or if it was because the tether was still firmly in place as she walked down the hall toward me, but nerves flooded my system. There was an energy in the air, a shift, and a hunger in me that wrestled my will before she'd even entered my chamber.

A soft knock sounded at my door, and I stood so fast that I knocked over the chair I was sitting in. I opened the door, and Sinna bowed. "Your Highness, I was told you requested my presence tonight."

I opened the door, and she stepped through, falling instantly into the more casual version of her that I'd gotten to know this past month. She walked around my room, picking things up and observing them, and I closed the door and locked it behind me.

"What happened?" she said finally. "Did Mel tire out early tonight?"

She was teasing me as I often complained about Melany and the show I put on for Ronan's sake, but tonight I didn't feel like joking. I was mesmerized by her presence and struck silent by how badly I wanted to touch her. She picked up the necklace off my vanity and brought it over for me to fasten.

"Wait," I said. "Let me try one thing." I turned her

by her waist and slid to the back of her neck, pulling her lips almost to mine.

The tether writhed inside me and I pulled away, grinding my teeth together in frustration.

"How?" I asked half out of breath. "How can you stand it?"

We'd spoken of many things, shared secrets that were best left unsaid, but I'd never addressed the tether so directly. She watched me carefully, and I could see in her clouded eyes the debate she was having about what she should disclose.

"Please," I urged.

She set the necklace down on the table and closed the gap between us taking my hands in hers. "It only hurts when you fight against it. Try giving in."

"I'm afraid." The words slipped out so quickly and I immediately wished I could take them back.

"Me too."

I slipped my hand to the back of her neck and felt my instincts pull away from the tether, the pain rising up, then I let go.

I pulled her lips to mine, letting the tether rush through me, exploding into a fierce sensation that jolted my body to life. Her arms wrapped around my neck, and I pulled her to my body by her waist. The kiss deepened, and I pushed her back onto my bed before I willed myself to break the kiss.

Hunched over, we fought to catch our breath, her eyes were wide, and her lips trembled. I took a step back, and she sat up quickly, covering her night-gown with her arm like a shield like it wasn't the same one she wore on all of our secret meetings.

My heartbeat slowed. "Put the necklace on," I demanded, fear echoing in my voice.

She scrambled for it, and I let her struggle with the clasp rather than help her, too afraid to get any closer. The tether dimmed, and I took a seat beside her on the bed.

"I don't know how you stopped us. If you're as strong-willed as they say. . . I don't think I could've. . ."

My body still pulsed with desire, even with the tether dulled. I needed to have her tonight. I reasoned with myself that this was the whole reason that I sought the necklace to begin with, so that I could safely have my way with her, without damaging my immortality.

What I felt when I kissed her without the tether concerned me. The sensation was more intense than the need to feed on blood. For the first time since we'd started our secret meetings, I doubted my will to resist her.

Luckily tonight I didn't have to.

THIRTY-TWO

I'd been warned with every kind of rhetoric about how dangerous the tether was. I'd even been practicing giving in so I could build up my tolerance, but when Maddox kissed me, and we had both given in at the same time, it was as if nothing else existed but him. For those precious few moments, there was no assassination, no courts, and no immortality.

That scared me.

I wanted nothing more than to stand up and run back to my room, but as much as I was struggling to compose myself, Maddox seemed equally vexed. I'd rushed to put on the necklace, desperate to dull the tether, but even after I put it on, something lingered.

Maddox's hair was tossed, his eyes red, his body tight with tension. If there was ever a time to coax him into sex, this was it. In all our time together, he hadn't laid a finger on me, and now he looked as if he was struggling not to devour me. I wanted it. I wanted it so bad that I was practically squirming out of my nightgown. This was just the plan. I promised I could keep myself from feeling longer than he could. It was time to prove it. I let my nightgown slip off my shoulder, and Maddox's eyes moved to it before he squeezed them shut, a pained look on his face. When his eyes opened again, they were filled with anger, his brow furrowed as he turned to me. I held my ground, challenging him to push it further with my eyes.

As long as the necklace was on me, it couldn't possibly be as dangerous as that kiss was.

He pushed me back onto the bed, grabbing the collar of my nightgown and tearing it down the middle. He pulled off his silky shirt and pants, his erection pulsing as he crawled over me. I sat up, startled by the suddenness, forgetting my supposed virginity as my body begged for his. He got to his knees, and he stole a kiss before he pulled my body to his. Losing myself, I wrapped my legs around him, and he pushed into me, sending a moan of pleasure echoing through his bedroom. My head rolled back as the pleasure overtook me, and he slid his hand up the back of my neck until my gaze met his. His white fangs glistened with hunger, the need reflected in his ember-glowing eyes.

As his dark tousled hair fell across one of his eyes, I couldn't see the monster. I could only see my mate. He only moved a fraction and the pleasure stacked, so I rolled my hips to push him deeper. He began to drive into me slowly, one godly thrust at a time, pulling an involuntary sound from my lips on each one. Chest to chest, his lips brushed mine. He ran his fangs gently across my neck, sending a chill through my body, and then he kissed me, driving harder into me.

The tether strained for release, fighting to break through the suppression of the necklace. Behind Maddox's eyes, I saw something I couldn't understand. Frustration, maybe? But what he did next made everything clear.

He kissed me as if in search of that feeling; The one that the necklace kept at bay.

He kissed me harder, timing it with a powerful push that started a frenzy in me. Without warning, he reached up and tore the necklace off of me, and the jewels scattered across his marble floors. We froze, my heartbeat synching with his as all the fear I should have felt blurred by desire.

The tether ignited, and I leaned forward and whispered against his lips, "Please."

He watched me so carefully I was afraid to breathe, then thrust into me. This time the necklace wasn't there to dull the pleasure from tearing through me. I lost control, my voice carrying, my hips driving him deeper. I burst into orgasm in seconds, my body shaking, with tears streaming down my face, but Maddox didn't stop. He held me, watching closely, driving into me again and again, until finally his body jerked and I felt his release explode inside me.

He buried his face into my chest and pulled me close. We collapsed, straining for air until we caught our breath. Then, with only a glance to acknowledge the line we'd crossed, we started again.

I awoke to the red-filtered light pouring through the window onto my face. Maddox's arms were wrapped around me, his breaths even and slow behind me. The tether flowed, and I felt the warmth of something new present in my chest. I was too afraid to move, too afraid to wake Maddox and put a permanent end to the loveliest night I'd ever had.

"You're awake," he said softly.

I sat up, turning to look at him, only to realize that he'd already been awake. He had already showered and changed into his day clothes. I rubbed my face. "Good morning."

He looked somber, his expression full of the same hard lines that were a permanent fixture on the Blood King, but rarely graced Maddox's face when we were alone. He lifted me and carried me to his bathroom, where a bath was already drawn. He lowered me into it, with no regard for his clothes getting wet. He sat on the edge of the tub then sighed. "I think we should stop this. We should take some time apart."

I wanted to tell him no, to pull him into the tub with me. I wanted to tell him we could endure it a little longer, but I was his assassin. The Hunter who would take his life. I didn't know how things had changed overnight. I held my tongue. When I didn't reply, he rubbed his hands together and stood, leaving me to soak with my thoughts.

I sank into the tub, my thoughts racing as the doubts about my mission crept in. Was I compromised? Was that why I insisted Finn to follow Ronan instead of me? What would Ezra say if she could see me now?

What was I thinking? Maddox drank the blood of innocents who were just trying to escape poverty. He lorded his court's strength over all the others,

BRITTNI CHENELLE

and his court nearly succeeded in wiping my court out completely--driving them into a hundred years of living underground. He was the devil, and yet, each time I closed my eyes, I could taste his lips and feel the threat of his fangs sweeping over my neck. My body perked with the memory.

If I was compromised, did that mean he was too? I splashed my face with water. If there's a Hunter in me, it was time for her to emerge.

I was in daze as I walked somberly to the dining room for breakfast. The other girls were already seated. It wasn't until the servants placed the dinner trays in front of me that I noticed Mel's scowl. But it was Celine's face that struck me.

Her eyes were dim and rimmed with darkness, her cheeks were sunken in and although she had a plate in front of her, she only pushed the food around with her chopsticks.

Before I could ask her what was wrong, Mel blurted, "You were with the King last night, weren't you?"

I exhaled before taking a bite of spicy cabbage. "Ronan was concerned the King was spending too much time with one tribute. If anything, it's a compliment."

Celine's mouth dropped open. "And he picked

220

YOU instead? He likes me the least?" Her eyes welled, and she began to cry.

"W-we don't know that. I think he just told Ronan to pick anyone else."

She shook her head, burying her face in her hands. "No," her breath skipped. "He hardly looks at me at all."

I wasn't sure if my words had eased Mel's worries or if she was reacting purely to help Celine feel better, but we both sprung into comfort mode. Even after Celine fell asleep with Mel and me stroking her hair, Mel's intensity never returned.

"Sorry," she said, her voice low as to not wake Celine. "I think all of this is making me crazy."

I nodded, my gaze moving back to Celine. "I think it's making us all crazy."

"You just don't understand," she said. "I love him."

I did understand. I understood more than I wanted to. Her words stung me, but instead of turning away, I needed to know more. "How do you know?"

She sighed and stared up at nothing in particular, her eyes distant. "I can't stop thinking about him. It's like. . . my body craves him or something. And immortality, that eternal gift that I'd come here seeking, it wouldn't matter unless he chose me. Does that make sense?"

All I could offer her was a nod. I stood and headed towards the door. "I'm going to get some rest. I'll be right next door if either of you needs me."

She smiled, her thoughts still adrift in her feelings for Maddox-- feelings she could embrace while I was forced to swallow them. I left the room feeling sorry for myself--turning my back on someone who truly needed me. Now I wondered if I could have endured Mel's feelings for Maddox for a few more hours, if Celine would have survived.

THIRTY-THREE

——— MADDOX ———

I spent the morning in the atrium among the blood thorns, the slow falling snowflakes punctuating my thoughts as I replayed the night before in my head and scolded myself for losing control. I'd known what Sinna was since she entered my court. I just planned to resist her longer. I wanted more of these perfect, beautiful moments. We'd only just begun, but the pull of a destined mate was far greater than I'd anticipated. Now the danger was real. I could feel it in my body, the rush of blood in my veins, my mortality looming. I'd lived too long to believe I could hide it. I'd seen immortal monarchs fall before. The moment a King's immortality fails, the sharks smell blood in the water. Would I have a week? A day? Or less? Would Sinna?

I wanted more time with her than I had counted on, the only loose end to an otherwise perfect plan.

If I spent time away from her, would my feelings dim? Was there any way to reset what had already been done? For once in my existence, my time was up, only it didn't bring me the comfort I thought it would. I picked a flower just as I had the night things started to change. I stared at it as the petals turned crimson. How had she bewitched me so completely, that for the first time in centuries I had the will to live? I should've sent her away before it was too late for her to escape.

A bone-rattling scream tore through the Blood Court. My skin felt on fire when I recognized the voice as Sinna's. I tore through the cathedral towards the sound and burst into the hallway where Ronan stared wide-eyed into Celine's bedroom. Before I reached him, I tasted Celine's blood in the air and saw the veins protruding from Ronan's neck as he restrained his urge to feed.

I turned to him, but his eyes looked through me. Several courtiers wandered into the hall, drawn to the scent of blood like flowers to sunlight.

"Don't let anyone in," I said, rushing in.

Melany sat at the foot of her bed, her gaze hollow, her face pale and clammy. She stammered and gave up on whatever she was trying to say, dropping her head and staring at the floor. The sound of running water drew my attention towards the bathroom, where blood mixed with water seeped onto the bedroom floor. The smell threatened to put my head in a fog, but fear for Sinna kept me alert.

I stepped into the bathroom, my eyes widening as the tub overflowed with Celine's blood, the tap still running over. Sinna held Celine's body to her chest, squeezing a blood-soaked towel around Celine's limp wrists.

She turned to me suddenly, her eyes widening.

"Help her, Maddox!" she screamed, her voice cracking, tears streaming down her face.

There wasn't a member of the Blood Court who would have reacted so strongly to a bloody death. It was practically built into our culture, but it was obvious Sinna had never witnessed anything quite so gruesome. I'd forgotten long ago that these were people, worth more than their blood or their company. Sinna's agony reminded me of that.

"What happened?" I said, finally.

"Bite her, Maddox! Change her! Make her immortal!"

"What happened, Sin?"

"She-she cut herself. She's out of time. Save her Maddox! Please!" she begged.

I stumbled back. "I can't."

She began to rock with Celine in her arms. "Why can't you? Do this for me."

"If she wants to die. . . I can't make her immortal. I won't. I'm sorry, Sin."

Celine's body convulsed, but I hadn't heard a heartbeat, not even when I first came in.

Sinna wiped her tears, smearing blood on her face. She rested Celine down on the floor and stood.

"Sin, I'm sorry." I reached for her, "Immortality is—"

She slapped my hand away. "I know very well what immortality is." She stared up at me, her brown and black flecked eyes bearing into me. "I'll never forgive you for this."

She pushed past me.

"Sin, please!"

I stopped short when I saw Ronan's face as Sinna pushed by him. His eyes narrowed, then he turned and hurried away. A mortal king is a dead king. I was surprised Ronan didn't rip me to shreds right there. If Sinna didn't leave now, she was going to die, and I was dead either way.

How could she expect me to imbue someone who

wanted to die with immortality? How, after I'd shared with her my own feelings on eternal life? It was a curse, an unnatural divinity given to those who deserve it least. The greedy, the power-hungry, and the envious. Mortals had loved ones to leave behind. Immortals were empty, and I was now somewhere between them. There was no time to make amends. I needed her to leave.

I went to her bedroom, knocking on the door and urging her to come out, but I heard nothing inside. The courtiers who usually avoided this part of the cathedral to avoid the temptation of the mortal tributes or to be beyond suspicion if one were to be found dead and drained, breezed casually through, their prying eyes all whispering the same thing, *time is up.*

I headed back to my room, hoping that Ronan might be able to coax her out, as long as I could convince him that he'd misinterpreted what he saw. I stopped short when I saw Ronan pacing outside my door, no doubt waiting for a private moment to interrogate me. I'd been so swept up with Celine's death and Sinna's anger that I'd allowed her to speak informally, with no regard to who was listening.

Ronan was no idiot. I'd have to be resolute in my argument to convince him not to wipe Sinna out immediately, or if his loyalty was in any way compromised and he didn't believe my lie, he might kill me instead.

He opened the door, following me inside my quarters and closing the door behind me.

"She's your mate, isn't she?"

"No. She is as unremarkable as the others."

He stepped closer. "Don't lie to me. I heard what she said."

"Her friend died. She was in shock, and she'll be punished and killed immediately for her disobedience. Bring her to me at once."

His fangs jutted out of his mouth. "There's talk of an uprising. The whole court thinks you're compromised."

"Now that I've explained that I am not, you should know we have nothing to fear."

He rubbed his hands over his face. "If you're lying about this, I'll—"

"You'll what? If you don't fall back in line, your disobedience will be dealt with, just as I will deal with Sinna's and anyone else who would question their king. You may consider this an opportunity to prove your loyalty. Bring the girl here immediately, and I shall drain her just like I did with Nova."

I could see in the sudden slump of his shoulders

that the mention of Nova had temporarily disarmed him. He'd had similar suspicions of her and confronted me in a similar manner, only to be proven wrong with a pale corpse.

His gaze filled with sadness. "Yes, Sire. I'll be right outside, just in case."

THIRTY-FOUR

— S I N N A —

I was all the way back to my room when I realized how covered in blood I was. I ran into my bathroom and tried to wash it off in the sink, while bile rose in the back of my throat. My throat was raw from screaming, my eyes red from crying. *Why, Celine?*

I'd never seen blood before. It was a terrifyingly bright substance that boisterously screamed how quickly a life was fading. In that desperate moment, I wanted to save her. I'd been so caught up in my own goals I wasn't there for her. If I had the power to save her, the power that Maddox was so hesitant to use, she'd still be alive. I stared at my blotchy face in the mirror, and no matter how long I looked, I didn't see a Hunter. Ferah was right. I'd gotten this far only to realize I didn't have what it took.

Movement behind me drew my attention. A dark shadow slithered across the tiles, weaving through my bloody footprints. The color deepened then rose out of the ground in a black mass. The black mist cleared, and Finn stood in front of me, his eyes filled with sorrow.

"She. . . she died."

He pulled me into his chest, and I let my legs go weak as he rubbed my back in circles. "I know."

He pulled back, his hands on both my shoulders and his jaw clenched. He exhaled through his nose, and then he said, "You need to make a choice Sinna. The vampires know you're the King's mate and the majority of them also believe the King is no longer immortal."

I stepped back, shaking his hands off me. "Are you sure?"

"Yes. They didn't know which of the tributes it was, since he spent a lot of time with Mel too, but after you yelled at the King, they were certain."

I wrung my hands. "Okay, so what do we do?"

"I think we should escape."

"W-what about the King? You just said he's mortal. I can kill him, and we can escape after."

He ran a hand through his hair. "Ferah hasn't responded to my correspondence. We don't have backup yet. Something's wrong. After everything with Celine. . . surely you're not considering trying to go through with the assassination."

I turned away, hoping to hide any pain that slipped onto my face.

"You've already done enough. It's too dangerous. I just heard the King say he was going to kill you himself. We don't have time. We have to go now."

I spun back around. "He said that?"

He nodded.

Why was I not surprised? I'd been told again and again how heartless the Blood King was. How did I allow myself to get so caught up in it and think I was somehow exempt from the slaughter? He hoarded immortality and slew anyone who sought it. He wouldn't even save my dying friend when I begged him. He let her die in my arms.

My blood boiled, my heart racing inside my chest. He thought he was going to kill me? He had another thing coming. "Let's finish the mission."

Finn licked his lips, his eyes never rising to meet me. "Is your immortality compromised, Sin?"

"No. Let's finish this. We kill him, and then we'll escape."

"I need to know the truth. If I go in there thinking you're safe and it turns out you are compromised, I might not be able to protect you. I need to know, Sin."

I crossed my arms over my chest. "I--I don't know for sure. I just know that if I don't do this, if I don't prove myself as a Hunter, I'll always regret it. This is my shot. Are you with me or not?"

His gaze struck me with intensity. "I've been with you the whole time."

The black mist rose up in his hand, dispersing to reveal his granite-hilted dagger- those used only by the Hunters.

I took it, steeling my nerves for whatever came next.

"We'll have to lay low for a little while. Hide in the woods until Ferah signals us that it's safe to return. Otherwise, we'll lead them right to our court, and we don't know how far along they are in their preparations."

"Got it." He placed his hand over the dagger and it dissolved into mist. "It'll be there when you need it," he said, brushing his thumb across my cheek. "As will I."

My heart hummed with anticipation as Finn melted into my shadow. I turned back to the sink and resumed washing the blood off my hands, only now my hands shook. A knock sounded at my door and my body tensed, as I slowly made my way to it. I pulled it open and Ronan glared at me, his formidable frame puffed up, and his nostrils flaring.

"The King has requested your presence immediately."

When he spoke, his fangs grew into sharp points. I bit down on the inside of my cheek to stop myself from cowering. I followed as he marched me to the King's bedroom, like a prison guard marching a prisoner to death row, but Ronan didn't know what I was.

I might be the King's mate, but I'm much more than that. I'm a Shadow Mage. I'm a Princess. I'm a sister. I'm a spy. And when the night is over, I'll be a Hunter too.

I am an executioner.

A King Killer, and no one will ever underestimate me again. I want Maddox to look me in the eye in his last moments and beg for his immortality while his life slips away. Only then will I be satisfied.

THIRTY-FIVE

— MADDOX —

I knew she was coming, but I was still stunned when she stepped into my chamber. She'd pulled her hair back into a ponytail. Her eyes were focused on me, but they didn't look at me with the same deference that they had before. They were ablaze with anger. I knew my decision to let Celine die had hurt her, and that she might not ever understand it, but I wasn't meeting with her to make amends.

I walked to my dresser and tossed her a rose that was sitting there, the one I'd given her the night before. She caught it, then jerked her hand back, dropping the blood thorn to the ground. Then I smelled it for the first time. Her blood. I walked over to her and took her hand in mine, wiping the red bead and staring in disbelief.

She loves me.

Her blood was the sweetest, most intoxicating scent I'd ever known, and I stepped back, frightened that I might break my promise and give in to the powerful temptation to taste her. Her cheeks bulged from her clenched jaw. A black cloud engulfed her hand, then cleared, leaving a dagger in its place. I walked to the door and locked it.

I took a deep breath and turned to face her.

"You don't seem surprised."

I put my hands in my pockets. "Why would I be surprised?"

"That I'm a Shadow Mage."

I grinned. "You may have a mortal father, but you could never pass as mortal. Plus, you look a lot like your parents. I met them once."

Her brow furrowed.

"I knew from the second you stepped into my court who and what you were."

She gritted her teeth. "You're lying. If you knew what I was, why didn't you kill me right there?"

"You're my mate."

"That's more of a reason. Why did you spare me? Did you pity me? Did you really think the great and powerful Blood King could withstand the pull of the tether? You got cocky, and now you'll die for it."

I couldn't help but smile at her as she worked herself up. I knew she needed to in order to complete her mission. "It wasn't that."

She stepped close to me and placed the dagger against my neck.

"Why then?" Tears slipped from her eyes, rolling down her soft cheeks.

I wanted to reach out and wipe them away. To kiss her and to reassure her, to take away some of the pain I caused. But she needed that pain.

"I wanted to. . . " The words got stuck in the back of my throat, my fear making them grow thicker. I swallowed hard.

She lowered her knife. "You wanted to what?" Her eyes widened. "To die?"

"I wouldn't expect you to understand."

"That's right. I don't."

"You haven't been alive as long as I have. You weren't there for the war."

She dropped her head. "So, your plan was to just let me... " She bawled her fist. "Make a fool out myself?"

"You came here to seduce and kill me, right? I figured it wouldn't hurt to let you. We both were getting what we wanted."

Her voice came out soft like a whisper. "Wanted?"

"The tether was stronger than I thought. Much stronger. I didn't expect things to happen so quickly. I wound up kind of wishing for more time. But this is it. This is all we get."

"So it's true then. You're not immortal anymore?"

I unbuttoned my shirt, pulling my shirt open to my exposed chest. "There's only one way to know."

She cried softly, her gaze never leaving mine.

"Do it." I urged. "Or have your shadow do it. You both need to get out of here. You have a sister to go home to, remember? I don't have anyone."

The door handle rattled, and my heart jumped up to my throat.

Sinna stepped closer, and I could see her shaking. "I... I can't do it," She said, sinking her face into my chest.

I wrapped my arms around her. "Then listen. You have to get out of here. Quickly. Please, Sin. You'll die here."

"They're going to kill you. Your own people. . . they're going to kill you."

"It's okay, Sin. Go."

"I can't."

Fuck. She's going to die, and it's my fault. How can I make her leave?

Ronan pounded on the door.

Panic settled in. "Please, Sin, please go."

Sinna's shadow grew, growing darker and rising from the floor like a cloud of ash. Sinna's arms tightened around me, "I won't leave you."

The familiar sensation of steel pierced my chest, and sliced through only inches from Sinna's head. Only this time, I felt the warmth of my blood as it slipped down my chest. I collapsed to the floor, stunned as the pain ate away at the corners of my vision. *So this is it? This time it's real.* A man pulled Sinna away as she screamed and fought, her arms reaching for me.

Mine instinctively reached for her, but her voice was muffled and fading fast.

Black ash consumed them, and they were gone, seconds before the door crashed open, and Ronan rushed in.

In his eyes, I did not see the traitor I'd expected. I did not see a man vying for the throne. There was only desperation and sorrow as he fought to slow the bleeding. I guess I was wrong about him. I wonder what other things I was wrong about.

I closed my eyes, pulling the memory of Sinna back to me as I lost everything else, bit by bit. I wouldn't change a thing, Sinna. I'd fall in love with you all over again. It might've been selfish, knowing

I'd corrupted your immortality as well. But you'll forget me and regain it in time. For now, at the moment of my death, you love me, and I wasn't wrong about how that might feel, except for one part.

I only wish we had more time.

THIRTY-SIX

*A*s soon as we made it out of the cathedral, we could hear footsteps behind us. My heart ached as Finn slipped us seamlessly through the shadows as only an expert Hunter could. Maddox was dead.

My mate.

Gone just like that.

I let my body go limp, relying fully on Finn's guidance to lead us to safety. I shuttered as I felt the tether waning, terrified that at any moment, I'd feel it go out completely. The sound of footsteps in the snow grew closer, and Finn's pace increased despite the fact that he already seemed winded. Was he scared of what he'd just done or what would happen to us if they caught us?

I didn't know. All I knew is there was still a tether. Maddox had known all along who I was. He fell willingly into love. I was no spy. I was no Hunter. I was nothing. I'd let down my sister, my people, and I lost my mate, trying to be something that I wasn't. Maddox might've been the things I accused him of.

He was careless with his life. . . with all life, and far too powerful for his own good. But, he knew who he was and what he wanted. My finger stung, so I popped in in my mouth, the iron taste of blood drawing my attention.

I loved him.

We'd hardly gotten any time at all, but it was more than most in the Shadow Court ever got.

Now that I knew what I was giving up, I no longer wanted to. I pressed my hand against my chest, hoping the tether wouldn't break. One more minute. Please, Maddox. One more minute.

Finn stopped short, interweaving us with the shadow of the nearest tree, and holding us completely still. A snow-white wolf crept through the moonlit forest, and we watched from the darkness where only Shadow Mages could dwell. The wolf moved closer, its nose twitching over the snow.

I held my breath. Could he smell us? We were

dead. The wolf approached our shadow and started pawing at the darkened snow. We were undetectable to the naked eye, but if he could smell us, he could follow us until we came out of shadow form. A soft whine floated out of the beast. I looked closely, his icy blue eyes jogging a memory. The night of the Moon ball, I'd spent the night dancing with those eyes, but in human form.

"King Herod?" I whispered.

The wolf nuzzled the snow and let out a low whine.

"Finn, I think he wants us to go with him."

"It could be a trap."

"You said yourself we can't go home. This might be our best chance."

Finn paused for a moment then nodded to me.

I watched the snowy creature as its gaze stared at the nothingness of our shadow, pacing around as its breath came out in white clouds around its muzzle.

"Alright, Your Majesty. Show us the way."

The giant puppy started back through the woods, toward the Moon Court, with the full moon hanging over us all to witness what unfolded next.

I held my breath and counted down each minute, urging Maddox through the tether to hang on for just one more each time. The wind howled around us, filling the night air with an eerie gloom that said this was only the beginning of something I couldn't yet understand. I was glad for it.

I was not a Hunter--but maybe if I could be brave enough, I could find out what I am.

AUTHOR'S NOTE

Thank you for reading *Chaste Blood*! Stay up to date on the release of *Chaste Moon, Repressed Royals: Book 2* by signing up to my newsletter.

Need more NOW? I have two COMPLETE trilogies available now!
NA Paranormal Romance: *The Fae & The Fallen*
YA Fantasy Romance: *Kingdom Cold*

I specialize in multicultural romances with a ton of angst and my favorite trope is enemies to lovers.

Special Shout out to my amazing PATRONS!
    Kisha Wilson
    Shelly Wilson
    Jeanette George
    Christopher J Canady
    Sabrina Jacklin

Made in the USA
Coppell, TX
09 January 2021

47827070R00146